THE ORPHAN'S SECRET DESTINY

ARABELLA LARKSPUR

CHAPTER 1

With the corner of her apron, Anna wiped the sweat from her brow.

She was hot already, and there was still so much more work to do. The sun had yet to rise, yet she had already been up for hours.

There was always something: fireplaces to clean out, set, and restart, and the general cleaning of the large townhouse she worked in.

It seemed there were fewer and fewer servants to help with the workload, and while Anna often asked the cook about this, she was vague in her response. Just the other day, the scullery maid had been let go, which meant more work for Anna. But there wasn't time to dwell on it now; that wouldn't get the work done.

. . .

She heard the gentle swish of skirts and knew that Mrs Harris, the housekeeper, had entered the room. That was about the only gentle thing about her.

For as long as she could remember, Anna always seemed to be the brunt of the housekeeper's sharp tongue. No matter what she did, it was never to Mrs Harris's standard. She was never working hard enough, never doing it well enough; her harsh words were a constant in Anna's busy life.

Anna felt her body tense as she waited for whatever Mrs Harris was going to say to her. It wasn't until the housekeeper grimaced to herself under her breath and turned to walk away that Anna realised she had been holding her breath.

She listened to the footsteps disappear into the distance, then sat back on her heels, taking a deep breath and trying to relax her shoulders again. She didn't understand why Mrs Harris didn't like her, but it had always been that way.

. . .

SHE FINISHED what she was doing, picked up her cleaning materials, and made her way into the kitchen, hoping she wouldn't run into anyone on the way.

As she reached the end of the hall, which led into the kitchen doorway, she could hear voices and stopped to listen. One of them belonged to the cook, Mrs Jones, and hearing her gentle voice made Anna smile.

In the way that Mrs Harris always seemed to find fault with her, Mrs Jones was completely the opposite. In fact, if it hadn't been for her, Anna often wondered what her life would have been like. Once the cook had finished talking, Anna heard another voice and realised it was the lady of the house, Eliza.

THEY ALL CALLED her the lady of the house, but she was really the daughter of the lord of the house. Eliza's mother had passed many years before, and even though Eliza was young when her mother died, she had started to take on the role her mother had left. Despite her young age, she had always been capable, and to Anna, even though Eliza was a few years younger than her, she always seemed so much older. She had a confidence and a self-assurance that made Anna admire her. Whereas some of the other younger servants often made snide comments about her, Anna was always quick to defend the young mistress.

As Eliza had grown older, she had taken on more and more of the running of the household.

Now, Anna could hear her discussing the menus she required with Mrs Jones. She knew that after speaking to the cook, Eliza would meet with Mrs Harris to organise the cleaning schedules and whatever else needed to be done over the course of the day and the coming week. Anna sometimes tried to imagine herself in Eliza's shoes, what it might be like to run a house, to be the one who gave orders rather than the one who took them.

SHE SHOOK HER HEAD, dismissing such a flight of fancy. She was just about to walk through the kitchen door when Eliza quickly came out. Anna nearly bumped into her and bowed her head quickly, dropping into a small curtsy and mumbling an apology under her breath.

"GOOD MORNING, ANNA," said Eliza.

ANNA BOBBED her head in greeting.

"Morning, ma'am," she replied, keeping her head bowed.

She listened as Eliza walked past and down the hallway before standing up straight and looking after her.

"COME ON, LASS," said Mrs Jones. "There's no time for mooning around; there's things to do."

Anna turned to Mrs Jones, who was smiling lovingly at her.

AS FAR AS Anna was concerned, Mrs Jones was the centre of everything in the house. She had always been like a mother to Anna, and she couldn't remember a time when the older woman wasn't in her life. Throughout the years, Mrs Jones had brushed away many a tear and given her many a gentle rebuke. Anna loved her, and she knew that, in her way, Mrs Jones loved her too. She smiled back and walked into the kitchen, ready to help wherever she could.

CHAPTER 2

*E*liza stayed silent, her head bowed over her plate, concentrating on the food before her as her father spoke. She could feel the frown starting to crease her forehead, and she took a deep breath, letting it out slowly, doing her best to settle her face into an expression as blank as possible.

No sooner had they both sat at the table and the servants had served the first course, than her father began talking about what he needed her to do around the house. I

t was as if he had no understanding of all that she did. As he went through his list, she could have ticked off almost every item, knowing she had it all in hand. But he seemed to take no notice.

He paid no attention to how she organised the staff and ran the house on a daily basis, and he took no notice now as she sat silently eating her meal.

In the past, she would respond, trying to reassure him that she had done everything he expected, but she learned a long time ago that he didn't listen to that either. So now she let him talk, sometimes nodding her head, but it was clear to her that he needed no interaction from her.

She was always aware of the servants in the room. While her father might not be listening, they certainly were. Every now and then, she would hear a small whisper among some of the younger servant girls. She never knew exactly what they said, and any conversation would stop as soon as they realised she was nearby. They would bob their heads, curtsy, and move on.

Though she didn't know what they were talking about, Eliza was always left with the uneasy feeling that there was something going on of which she was unaware. She had wondered whether this evening would be the moment she gathered her courage and asked her father about it, but as he continued to speak, barely stopping between mouthfuls of food, she realised it wouldn't be tonight.

As plates were cleared away and each course was served, Eliza did her best to remain calm and enjoy the meal.

She had a vague memory that it hadn't always been like this. She had been but a child when her mother left them to join the angels, but every now and then she would have short flashes of tinkling laughter, followed by her father's deeper laugh as they all shared a meal together.

She often wondered what things would have been like if her dear mother were still with them, then pushed the thoughts away and forced a small smile to her lips as her father glanced in her direction.

For a moment, he seemed to catch himself, and Eliza knew exactly what he was thinking. She had seen paintings of her mother and was aware of the significant resemblance between them. Every now and then, her father looked at her as if he were seeing a ghost from his past. But Eliza knew she was no ghost. He was seeing her, but for a moment, he saw his wife in his daughter's face.

Almost before he could stop himself, he smiled, and Eliza knew that the memories she had of a smiling and laughing father when her mother had been around weren't a figment of her imagination. Then, just as quickly, his smile disappeared as he realised that it wasn't his wife, the woman he had loved for many years, but his daughter, who sat across the table from him.

Eliza tried not to wince at the obvious disappointment that flashed across his face before he looked down at his meal and continued talking.

CHAPTER 3

The fact that her father had been up until almost dawn in his study was not lost on Eliza. It had been this way for a number of nights now, and she would find herself lying in bed awake, listening for his footsteps as he walked down the hall past her bedroom to his own.

She didn't know what he did, but in the mornings, his desk was often covered with paper and ink. Her guess was that he was writing letters, though to whom, she didn't know.

She sighed as she walked into the kitchen looking for Mrs Harris, the housekeeper. She saw her standing with Mr. Smith, the steward, and unaware of Eliza's presence.

Her usual pinched expression was on her face as she spoke to some of the other servants.

Mrs Harris turned at Eliza's voice, and the smile and pleasant expression she always had for the young mistress quickly replaced her earlier scowl.

"Yes, Miss?" she replied and walked over to where Eliza waited.

"My father's study needs cleaning," Eliza said. "Can you send one of the servants to go in and get it done this morning?"

Her eyes searched the small group of young women and stopped when they reached Anna.

"Actually, send in Anna," she said and turned on her heel, walking back out of the kitchen before Mrs Harris could say anything.

"Well, you heard her," Mrs Harris said to Anna, her voice short. "Hurry up and get it done. You still have everything else that you need to finish today, and then I need you in the scullery. There'll be dishes to clean and whatever other help Mrs Jones needs," she said and then followed in Eliza's direction out of the kitchen.

Anna did her best not to sigh and wondered why Mrs Harris couldn't ever be polite, at the very least.

She felt Mrs Jones' eyes on her and forced a smile under her watchful gaze.

"I'm going," she said as she collected the cleaning materials she would need and walked towards HIs Lordship's study.

As she walked in, she could see why it needed cleaning and tidying.

It was a mess, papers everywhere, ink smudges, and soot from the fireplace. She'd heard some of the older staff talking about how Lord Harrow had been spending many late nights in his study, working at his desk.

While they'd always been told that someone should be on hand if either the lord or the mistress was still awake, Anna knew that Lord Harrow had been sending the servants to bed.

She could see where he fed the fire himself, leaving its surroundings in a mess.

On his desk were glasses of half-drunk liquid, and as Anna collected them, sticky rings had formed on the wood beneath.

Everything needed a good clean, but first, she set about tidying and putting everything away. After having worked here for so long, she knew where everything belonged.

She'd been taught to put things away without looking at anything too closely, and so, while she could read, she always worked hard to avert her gaze.

She knew that many things in His Lordship's office were important and confidential, and while some of the other servants were happy to gossip about anything they came across, that wasn't Anna's way.

She'd never known her mother or her father. The townhouse in London that she worked at was the only home she'd ever known.

She'd asked Mrs Jones when she was younger to explain how she'd come to be here, and the cook had always promised that she would tell her when she was older, but it seemed to Anna that she was never old enough to hear whatever information Mrs Jones knew.

In the end, she'd given up asking.

Perhaps it didn't matter.

Perhaps it was enough to know that her mother had passed so long ago that she had no memory of her and that her father, whoever he was, had never wanted to claim her as his daughter.

Because of that, she was always thankful for the place that she had here.

It had been Lord Harrow's wife, Lady Harrow, who'd always reassured her that this was her home.

She'd been a beautiful and kind woman from what Anna could remember, and she could see Eliza's growing resemblance to her. Lord Harrow had always been distant, and Anna assumed it was due to his standing in society. Dealing with the servants was beneath him, and he'd left it to Eliza and to his wife before her. But Anna still felt a sense of loyalty and she took her time now making sure that his study was clean and organised.

AS SHE WAS WIPING down his desk, doing her best to remove the marks that had been left on the top of it, she noticed that there had been spills down the side as well and over the front drawers. As she rubbed at the stains, her hand grazed some kind of lever or button that was standing proud of the rest of the wood near one of the desk drawers.

Without realising it, she triggered something and a small drawer popped out. It was one that she'd never noticed before. It was full of papers; some looked like important legal documents, and amongst those there was a small pile of letters tied together with a piece of yarn.

STARTLED, Anna jumped back slightly and before she knew what she was doing, she was reading the writing on the envelopes of the letters and scanning the documents next to them. What she read shocked her.

Fearful of being caught, she just picked out information, expecting to hear somebody come through the door at any moment. The writing on the envelopes was obviously the pretty florid script of a woman, and they were all addressed to His Lordship.

The documents, from her quick look, seemed to mention a child, but it was clear that it wasn't Miss Eliza they were talking about. The mother of the child mentioned was not the late Lady Harrow.

Anna was lost in reading the papers, not realising what she was doing. She had picked up the documents, trying to discover the truth of their meaning. It was only when she heard Lord Harrow's voice barking a command to one of the male servants that she caught herself.

She quickly stuffed the papers back into the drawer she had found them in and closed it with her knee. She heard the mechanism she'd originally triggered click as it went back into place. Just as she straightened herself up, Lord Harrow walked through the door.

"WHAT ARE YOU DOING IN HERE?" he said, his voice angry.

He looked at her suspiciously, and she wondered whether he knew what she'd been doing. She reminded herself that there was no chance he could have known. He hadn't seen her; she'd made no noise; he'd been outside. Yet the guilt that she might have been caught doing something she knew she shouldn't have washed over her. Her cheeks reddened, and she bowed her head, averting her eyes from his gaze.

. . .

"I'M JUST TIDYING your desk, my lord. Mrs Harris asked me to come in and clean in here for you."

"WELL, it looks like you're done. Off you go," he said.

When she didn't move straight away, his voice grew louder and angrier.

"Off you go, I said! I don't want you coming back in here. This is my private study. I don't need you nosing about my things. I know what you servants are like."

AS HIS COMMAND turned into a rant, Anna quickly gathered all her cleaning things and hurried out the door, down the hall, down the stairs, and towards the kitchen. By the time she got there, she was slightly out of breath.

"WHAT IS IT, MY GIRL?" Mrs Jones asked. "You look a state. What's happened?"

THE WORDS she had read in the documents raced through her mind, and she longed to tell somebody about them, to try to make sense of it all. But she didn't think Mrs Jones was the right person.

"I'M FINE, Mrs Jones. I was just cleaning His Lordship's study and he came in. He was a bit angry."

"WELL, HE'S A BUSY MAN," the cook said. "I imagine you were just in his way." She smiled at her gently, and Anna nodded.

But she was unable to get Lord Harrow's face out of her mind.

She had never seen him quite like that before. As he had spoken to her, his face had reddened, and his voice had grown angrier.

His last words, warning her to stay out of his office, rang in her ears.

CHAPTER 4

*E*liza looked out of the window onto the busy street below.

Ladies walked along the pavement together in twos or threes, their pace casual as Eliza watched them talking.

Everyone else around them seemed to bustle past at a hurried pace.

She could see housemaids with baskets of laundry and young women in plain-looking dresses with baskets of flowers, doing their best to sell their wares to the ladies Eliza had been watching enviously.

It seemed she didn't ever have time to please herself.

While she had other young women she saw in

social settings, there wasn't really anyone she called a close friend.

After their period of mourning, her father had entertained every now and then, but these occasions had become less frequent.

Now, Eliza couldn't remember the last time they had people over for supper. In fact, the only regular visitors they seemed to have were her father's advisors. These were two older men who, while polite, rarely spoke with Eliza and often entered her father's study as soon as they arrived.

She never knew what they spoke about, though every now and then her curiosity would get the better of her, and she would stand by the closed study door, trying to hear through the thick wood. She could make out the different voices as each man spoke, but it was unclear what they were saying.

More recently, after any visit, her father would be in a foul mood. She had noticed more and more the frown that settled on his face and the shortness of his words. If anyone did anything or said anything he wasn't happy with, his temper would flare. Eliza always tried her best to stay out of his way during these times as much as possible.

So when she heard the opening and closing of her father's study door and his advisors' footsteps, she walked quickly over to a chair and sat down, pulling out some needlework and trying to look busy.

She didn't hear her father come out of his study, so she was taken by surprise when she looked up to see him standing in the doorway, his eyes resting upon her.

Once again, she noticed his usual frown soften.

"I NEED to speak with you, Eliza," he said.

SHE PUT THE NEEDLEWORK DOWN, expecting him to come into the room and join her.

"NO, IN MY STUDY," he said, and the frown returned to his face as he turned on his heel and walked away.

She got up and did her best to straighten out the creases in her skirts before following him.

"CLOSE THE DOOR," he said.

She walked in and, when she turned back around to face him, he was standing by the fire.

This room had always been dark, with rich colours and dark wood. Eliza knew that her mother had decorated the rest of the house, but this room she had left to her father's discretion, and it was bare of any feminine touch.

Sometimes she could smell the tobacco that he smoked, but she never came in here unless invited, and that wasn't very often.

"Yes, Father?"

Lord Harrow cleared his throat.

"Sit down, Eliza," he said, pointing in the direction of a chair near where he stood.

She sat down, looking up at him and waiting.

"You're 18 now," he said to her, "and really it's time that you were married."

Before she could say anything, he continued,

"I have found a match for you. An old friend of mine, Lord Whitfield. I'm sure you know him. He's a recent widower; he has two small children, and I know that he will soon be looking for a wife to help him take care of them. I have arranged for a formal introduction for the two of you."

As soon as he finished speaking, her father turned back towards the fire, and she felt strangely like she was being dismissed.

She couldn't quite believe the words she had just heard.

This was the first time her father had ever spoken to her about marriage.

She assumed that it was something that would happen one day, but having never had the opportunity to spend time with any of the gentlemen she knew of, she'd barely given it much thought.

To hear that this was not the case for her father and that he had not only been considering it but had already found her a prospective husband was quite a shock.

She waited for him to turn around, unsure what to say, wanting to question him but also nervous of the short temper she knew was often just under the surface. When he didn't move or say anything more, Eliza got up and walked over to the study door. Her hand hovered over the handle as she still considered turning and saying something.

"He's a good man, Eliza,"

It was the first time she'd heard gentleness in her father's voice for a long time.

She heard him walk towards his desk and then the creak of the chair as he sat down in it. A moment later, she heard the scratching of the pen on paper, and she knew that there was nothing more to be said.

She opened the door and walked out, closing it silently behind her before leaning against it, trying to gather her thoughts. She closed her eyes and took a few deep breaths.

What of love? she thought.

This was not the kind of marriage arrangement she had imagined for herself. And to be promised to a friend of her father – he would be an old man. She could feel herself grimacing at the thought. She opened her eyes and saw Anna standing before her.

"Are you alright, miss?" Anna asked, dropping into a small curtsy.

Eliza had always liked Anna. While she was slightly older than herself, it had always felt very much like they'd grown up together. Like Mrs. Jones the cook and Mrs. Harris the housekeeper, Anna had been a constant in Eliza's life, and she found comfort in that.

"Yes, I'm fine, Anna," she said.

Anna raised her head.

"Shall I get you some tea, miss?" she offered.

"That's a lovely idea," Eliza said, and she walked into the sitting room.

She sat down on the chair she'd been in previously and picked up the needlework she had discarded when her father had come in just a moment ago.

She looked down at the image she was creating on the clean white linen, but she couldn't concentrate. When she heard Anna come into the room with the tea tray and place it down on the table, she realised she had added nothing to the picture since she sat down.

She listened as the tea was poured into the cup and then brought over and placed into her hands. She didn't realise she was shaking until she heard the cup rattle in its saucer. Anna took it from her and placed it on the table beside her.

"I'll leave it here for you, miss," she said, smiling gently. "You can have it when you're ready."

Eliza nodded, grateful for her presence.

"Will there be anything else, miss?" Anna asked.

Still unable to speak, Eliza shook her head and heard rather than saw Anna bob quickly and leave the room.

She reached over to pick up the teacup and saucer once more, but again it rattled noisily as soon as she lifted it from the table.

She placed it back down.

. . .

Anna walked back down to the kitchen, her heart going out to Eliza. She had overheard some of the servants talking about a conversation between Lord Harrow and his advisors. T

here was talk of a marriage for Miss Eliza, a marriage between her and one of Lord Harrow's friends, Lord Whitfield.

Anna couldn't think who he was and wondered whether she knew him; perhaps it was the same for Eliza.

Listening more closely to the conversations between the servants, especially the male servants, since her discovery in Lord Harrow's study, Anna wondered whether perhaps somebody else knew of the hidden papers and letters she had found. She tried to piece together the small fragments of information she gathered from the papers themselves, and all sorts of conclusions about what they might mean raced through her mind.

. . .

She hadn't heard anyone else mention anything about them, and she said nothing about finding them. Every now and then, she would find herself walking past his study, wondering if she would be able to slip in and read the papers more closely. However, the lord's warning kept coming back to her.

Whatever Lady Harrow may have said about her always having a home there, Lady Harrow was no longer with them. Anna wasn't sure that the lord would be as generous, especially if he caught her disobeying him.

CHAPTER 5

*A*nna could see that Eliza was nervous, but she had bitten her tongue, unsure what to say to ease her concerns.

Lord Whitfield was coming for tea; it was the formal introduction that Lord Harrow had spoken about.

Ever since he had confirmed the date, Anna had watched as the young lady of the house had become quieter, throwing herself into the household duties that she had taken on as her own.

In the past, Anna and Eliza had shared a few quiet moments together.

As Eliza had grown into a young woman, Anna had become almost a part-time lady's maid to her.

There wasn't enough staff in the house for that to be a full-time role, but in those moments when she drew the young mistress's bath or helped her dress or with her hair, they would share small conversations.

Anna knew she was just a servant and understood her place, but in those moments, it was obvious that Eliza missed not only the guidance of a mother but also the comfort of a friend. The young woman barely left the house, and the family had visitors less and less.

"I've heard that Lord Whitfield is a kind man," Anna said carefully.

She wanted to reassure Eliza without crossing the invisible line that she knew lay between them.

Eliza sighed.

"Yes, I've heard the same thing," she replied to Anna and smiled. "It's just that this isn't how I imagined marriage would be," she confided. "My father hadn't mentioned any prospects before now, and while I knew that he would have a say in who became my husband, I didn't think that would mean I would have none."

Anna nodded, not knowing how to respond to such openness.

This wouldn't be the kind of conversation that was encouraged between a servant and the lady of the house, but Anna was aware of how unique the situation was.

Eliza had no mother and no friends. She had her father, of course, but other than him, the only people she saw regularly were the staff in the house.

Anna realised that it was her Eliza saw most of all.

"I do wish my mother was here. I'm sure things would be so different if she was, and even if they weren't, I just know that she would have the right words and help me to do the right thing."

Anna knew exactly what Eliza meant.

She often missed the fact that she had no mother

of her own, and while Mrs Jones, the cook, was really the next best thing, it wasn't the same.

She had no experience of it herself, but she'd heard some of the other servants talk about their relationships with their own mothers, and as she listened to their words, she always felt a deep longing. People would say that you can't miss what you've never had, but that wasn't Anna's experience.

"I'M SO SORRY, ANNA," Eliza said quickly. "You also lost your mother at a young age. It's insensitive of me to complain about my own situation."

ANNA APPRECIATED THE CARING WORDS.

"It's okay, miss," she said. "It's not insensitive. It's right that you would have missed your mother. She was a kind woman, from what I remember."

"DO YOU REMEMBER YOUR OWN MOTHER?" Eliza asked, then realised what she'd said. "I'm so sorry. You don't need to answer that. That was very forward of me."

. . .

ANNA CHUCKLED, trying to put Eliza at ease.

"No, it's okay, miss. No, I don't remember her at all. I'm told she passed not long after I was born, so I don't suppose I would. I don't really know anybody who knew her, or at least no one talks about her, so I don't even have anybody else's memories either."

"I OFTEN WISH that my father would talk about my mother more. I thought perhaps once our period of mourning was over that he would, but it's never happened, and I've never felt like I could ask."

THE TWO YOUNG women looked at each other, both understanding the unspoken loss they shared and bonding over it for a moment. Then Anna remembered her place.

"Are you happy with your hair like this, miss?" she asked, changing the subject.

ELIZA LOOKED in the mirror at her reflection and nodded.

It didn't much matter, she thought. He was going

to be an old man, and it's not like she had a choice in any of it.

"It looks lovely, Anna. Thank you," she said.

Eliza remained seated even after Anna had left the room. She didn't know how long she sat there, staring into the mirror.

A gentle knock on the door and Anna's return to announce the arrival of Lord Whitfield brought her back to her senses. Taking one last look at herself, she got up and made her way downstairs to the sitting room where he was waiting. He stood as she entered the room, giving her a small bow and greeting.

"Good afternoon, Miss Harrow," he said with a smile.

Eliza was surprised by how handsome he was. She had expected someone who looked similar to her father, but the man who greeted her was very different. His smile was kind, and so was the look he gave her.

. . .

"Good afternoon, Lord Whitfield," she replied. "Would you like some tea?"

They both sat down as tea was served. Today, Eliza's hands were steady as she took the cup and saucer offered to her. She made polite conversation about the weather and his children. After those niceties had been exhausted, she was quite at a loss as to what to say next.

"I understand this must be difficult for you, Miss Harrow," he said. "Going through this without your mother must be very hard."

Eliza wondered what her father had said to him. Certainly, it seemed he hadn't mentioned that this potential marriage was all his idea and that she had no say in it at all.

Of course, it was difficult without her mother, but she knew that even if her mother were here, having her marriage arranged for her and not having any say in it at all would not have been any easier.

She couldn't say these things to him, of course, so she just nodded.

"I miss my wife very much," he admitted. "If it weren't for my children, I don't think I would be looking for another wife. I loved her dearly, and it is a lot to ask to find that again."

Eliza wasn't sure exactly what he was trying to say to her, and he didn't say anything more.

They finished their tea, he said his goodbyes, and took his leave.

Before he left, he asked if he could call on her again. She hadn't found the experience of being with him as awful as she'd expected. Not that it made a difference, but she agreed and said she would like that very much. Once he had gone, it was Anna who came in to collect the tea tray and take it away.

"He does seem very nice," Eliza said to her. "More handsome than I expected, and he seemed kind."

. . .

"Kindness is a good thing, ma'am," Anna agreed.

Over supper that evening, Lord Harrow mentioned the visit. He didn't ask Eliza what she thought or how she felt but just remarked that he was glad Lord Whitfield had come over and seemed pleased with Eliza.

She was starting to feel like a piece of property and wished she understood why she was being forced to marry a man she barely knew, who was so much older than her.

It was clear her father would brook no argument, and there was no ability to discuss it at all.

Whatever else, Eliza loved her father, and so she said nothing when the meal finished, and he excused himself and disappeared into his study. She was left on her own, as on almost every other evening for as long as she could remember.

"I wish I knew what he did in that study of his all night," she said to Anna as she drank her tea later in the sitting room.

The fire was blazing, and the room always looked soft by its light, but she couldn't miss that during the day, parts of their furnishings were starting to look a bit shabby.

She hadn't ever noticed before, but as she got older, she started to become more aware. She wondered whether her father's advisors coming over so often and him spending so much time in his study was just about him dealing with the business of their estate. It wasn't something she ever understood, but perhaps he was busy planning the redecoration of some of the rooms.

Anna said nothing in response to Eliza, though she started to wonder whether her discovery in Lord Harrow's desk was something she should share with her.

"Do you know what he does in there?" Eliza turned and asked Anna. "You clean and tidy in there during the day. Can you tell?"

. . .

Anna hadn't been in there since that day when Lord Harrow had almost shouted at her to never enter the room again.

"I haven't been in there for a while," she admitted. "Your father has told me that he doesn't want me in there anymore."

"That's strange," said Eliza. "That seems very secretive. It makes me want to go in there and find out what he's hiding."

Before Anna could stop herself, her head was nodding in agreement. She cleared her throat and, before she changed her mind, told Eliza about the small drawer she'd found in her father's desk and the papers within it.

"I wasn't looking, you understand, ma'am. I was just cleaning, wiping it down. Everything was so sticky. Anyway, I was just wiping it down, and I must have accidentally touched something, and before I knew it, well, there was a drawer I'd never seen before. It popped open, and there were documents in there, and what looked like letters. I didn't read them," she said, "but maybe that's what your father's doing in there."

As soon as the words were out of Anna's mouth, she regretted them.

She looked at Eliza's face, trying to gauge how she'd taken the information.

She hadn't been completely honest because, while she hadn't read the documents completely, she had tried to read them as much as she possibly could. She'd certainly seen more than she knew His Lordship would have liked.

But rather than looking angry or like she was going to rebuke her, Eliza's eyes widened in curiosity.

. . .

"You must have seen something on the documents, something that would give us a clue as to what they were about."

Anna didn't miss that Eliza said "us" and not "you." It seemed already that the young mistress was looking to join in on solving the mystery.

CHAPTER 6

Over the next few days, the two young women discussed the papers that Anna had discovered in Lord Harrow's study. Through snippets of conversation, they tried to piece together what the documents and hidden letters might mean.

Anna, still unsure of how much to tell Eliza, kept quiet about what she'd read. It was obvious that Eliza wanted to go into the study and try to trigger the mechanism that would open the drawer, but finding a good time was difficult. Since their initial conversation, Lord Harrow had been spending even more time in his study, and neither of them knew when an opportunity to go in and have a look might materialise.

. . .

ADDING TO THAT, it seemed that Mrs Harris was on a warpath.

If Anna had thought that the housekeeper didn't like her before, it was very clear now.

Every time she saw her, Mrs Harris had another list of things for her to do or places for her to be, and most nights, by the time she made it upstairs to her small room, she was exhausted. On some mornings, she would come down to the kitchen, and it would just be her and the cook, Mrs Jones.

There had been more than one occasion when their shared morning cup of tea resulted in tears as Anna tried to understand Mrs Harris' behaviour towards her.

"Is it that I've done something wrong, Mrs Jones? I've tried so hard to do everything she asks, and I do it to the best of my ability. But it seems no matter what I do, she's never happy with me. She doesn't seem to be like this with any of the other servants, and she's certainly always so pleasant towards the mistress. I mean, of course she would be; I understand it's different for her, but I just don't know what I can do."

. . .

THE WORDS TUMBLED from Anna as she sat at the kitchen table with Mrs Jones, drinking a cup of tea and eating a slice of bread and jam.

Even now, she knew that it wouldn't be long before the housekeeper was up, and if she came in and saw Anna sitting here, she would be displeased. It didn't matter that it was earlier than she usually was up.

It seemed nothing mattered to Mrs Harris except that Anna was working all the time. She'd noticed that even on her monthly Sunday off, once they'd all been to church together, Mrs Harris would still ask her to come back to the house and do some extra work. The list of things that needed doing seemed to be endless.

ANNA USUALLY AGREED. The truth was, she had nowhere else to go.

On occasion, she would walk through the streets, but it always felt like an unwelcome place. If she stayed near the house, she would see the local ladies and gentlemen strolling together, sometimes arm in arm. Other times, she would see other servants from the nearby townhouses.

But if she dared to venture further away, the

people in the streets seemed wild and unsafe. Their clothing was patched and ragged, they often looked dirty, and many times she'd come across people who'd obviously had accidents and lost legs or eyes.

She'd even seen one young man with a small hook where one of his hands should have been.

She shivered at the memory.

Above all, it was the smell—it just smelled terrible.

And so, with that her only choice on a Sunday afternoon, coming back to the townhouse to work seemed a far better option.

Anna knew that could so easily be her and part of her concern with how Mrs Harris treated her was an underlying fear that she was just a few angry moments away from finding herself living amongst that filth.

Mrs Jones reached across and patted Anna's hand. It was only then that Anna realized she'd been so lost in thought she'd forgotten where she was.

"You'll be alright, lass," Mrs Jones said. "I'm sure Mrs Harris means nothing by the things she says. It's hard running a house, organizing all you young ones, and making sure everything gets done. I think there's a lot more she's had to do since her ladyship passed. I know the mistress tries to step into her mother's shoes, but I think Mrs Harris has taken on a lot of responsibility, and you know how his lordship can be."

Anna nodded, remembering how he had shouted at her. She knew exactly how his lordship could be, though in truth that had been her first experience of it, and she would prefer it didn't get repeated and that it would be her last.

She tried to agree with what Mrs Jones said about Mrs Harris, knowing she would never understand all the things a housekeeper had to do.

In many ways, she was grateful not to have the responsibility.

She sighed.

"I'll just try harder," she said to Mrs Jones. "I'll just try to do everything Mrs Harris says and do it even better."

. . .

"That's a good girl," Mrs Jones said to her. "Now, you'd better get started before she comes in and sees you sitting here with me."

The cook gave her a gentle smile.

Anna didn't know what she would do if Mrs Jones wasn't there, and she smiled back thankful for the older woman's wise words.

If it wasn't for the fact that she was able to speak to her about these things, it would be so easy to be like some of the other servants, gossiping amongst themselves, and she knew that she didn't want that. Any opinions that they might give her wouldn't help her, and she was sure that she would just become bitter and angry about her lot. Mrs Jones always helped her to see how much she had to be grateful for.

Anna was upstairs cleaning one of the many bedrooms when Eliza came in to speak to her.

. . .

"I've been looking for you everywhere, Anna," her voice was excited. "Father's going out tonight. He's going to see someone or other about something. I didn't really listen after he said he was going out. All I could think about was the fact that we could get into his study and have a look at those papers. What do you think?"

Anna could feel a mixture of excitement and nerves in her stomach at the thought of going into His Lordship's study after being told never to enter there again. But if he was going to be out of the house, and if she was going to be with Miss Eliza, then perhaps it would be okay.

She was still curious to know what the documents meant. Her skim reading of them had raised more questions in her mind than answered them, and she couldn't get the image of the pile of letters tied up with string addressed to His Lordship out of her mind.

What did any of it mean, she wondered.

"Please say yes," Eliza said. "Please say you'll come in with me."

. . .

The look on her face and the pleading in her voice was something that Anna couldn't refuse, and she nodded her head.

"Okay, Miss."

Eliza told her what time and where to meet her later that night. It would be late, but Anna was used to that.

They stood in front of the desk. Anna had a small lamp in her hand. Even though the house was quiet and everyone had gone to bed, they were still nervous about being seen. Thus, it was by this dim light that they'd made their way into the study.

Now that they were there, it was almost as if both of them were too nervous to go any further, worried about what they might find, though for very different reasons.

"Shall I open it, Miss?" Anna whispered.

. . .

ELIZA NODDED SLOWLY, and Anna reached under the desk beside the drawers, trying to remember exactly what she'd done last time. Her hand brushed back and forth, trying to find a small button. Eventually, she found it and pressed it.

Just like before, the small drawer, which was normally hidden, popped out. The contents looked exactly the same as she'd left them, and she wondered whether Lord Harrow ever opened the drawer and looked inside himself.

THE TWO YOUNG women looked at the documents and then at each other before turning their attention back to the papers. Eliza reached out tentatively and picked them up, while Anna held the lamp as closely as she could. The two of them read the papers silently.

ANNA HEARD a sharp intake of breath as Eliza took in what they said.

The papers spoke about a child—an illegitimate child. It wasn't completely clear who the father was, but Anna assumed it was Lord Harrow, and from Eliza's reaction, it was clear she assumed the same.

The mother wasn't mentioned. Who the child was, or where they were now, was also not mentioned. There was a date, but the ink had smudged, and it wasn't clear.

When they had read everything, they stood there in stunned silence, neither knowing what to say to the other, but both with their thoughts racing.

Eliza put the documents back in the drawer and then picked up the pile of letters. There were at least half a dozen, and both of them knew they wouldn't have time to read them tonight.

"I'm sure my father will be back soon," Eliza said. "We should go."

She closed the drawer, and the two young women made their way out of the study. When they had closed the doors behind them, they looked at each other but said nothing.

. . .

"Let's talk in the morning," Eliza said. "Off you go to bed. You take the lamp; I'll be fine."

Anna nodded and made her way to the kitchen to walk up the stairs towards her room.

Eliza stood watching her, trying to piece together what she'd read and make sense of it all.

An illegitimate child, she thought. Obviously, her father's illegitimate child. Where were they now, she wondered, and what did it all mean?

Once Anna was gone from her sight, she turned and made her way to her own bedroom.

CHAPTER 7

*D*iscovery of the documents seemed to awaken a curiosity in Eliza. She wondered whether she was using it as a distraction from the knowledge that she knew one day, probably sooner rather than later, she would have to marry Lord Whitfield. Whatever the reason, she often sought out Anna and encouraged her to help search the house.

She wasn't sure whether she would get another opportunity to go into her father's study, though she longed to read the letters she had seen in the drawer next to the other papers. She was certain there would be more information inside—information about the child that the documents had mentioned.

Of course, none of it made sense. She knew from what she'd been told that her parents had been deeply in love. The idea that her father would have betrayed her mother in this way wasn't something she thought could be true.

THE ONLY ALTERNATIVE was that this child, her father's child of whom she knew nothing, was older than she was.

Perhaps it was a situation that had occurred before her father and her mother were married. If that was the case, it called into question everything Eliza believed about herself. There was somebody out there who was her brother or sister, and not only were they her sibling, but if they were older than her, they would be the rightful heir to everything that her father owned and was.

IT WAS that personal revelation that kept her awake at night and made her wonder whether trying to find out more was really in her best interests. If she had no inheritance, then she truly had no choice but to marry Lord Whitfield. Whether it had been her father's decision or not, she would have nothing of her own and, like so many women, would be reliant on a husband to provide for her.

Despite those thoughts filling her with dread, the idea of having a sibling, perhaps finding out who they were and getting to know them, felt more like a blessing and a gift than any physical or financial loss that might entail.

Anna was dealing with her own thoughts about their discovery. When she had seen the papers herself before she spoke to Eliza about them, it was the information about a child that had caught her attention. When she first read the words, it had suddenly made her aware of how little she knew about her own parentage.

She had parents, of course, but all she knew was scant information about her mother, and really all that was, was that she had died when Anna was just a baby. How she had ended up here had always been foggy in her mind.

Whenever she'd asked anybody about it, she'd heard different variations.

One said she had been left on the doorstep; another that she'd been the child of a friend of Lady Harlow.

Who her father was had never been spoken about, and while Mrs. Jones had promised that she would tell her all about who her parents were when she got older, so far the information had never been passed to her.

AFTER THE DISCOVERY of the documents, Anna wondered whether now was the time to speak to the cook. Perhaps if she mentioned what she'd read, it would open up a conversation, and she would finally know where she came from.

But she knew that the information they had discovered could be seen as dangerous.

Talk of His Lordship having an illegitimate child would only cause gossip, and that would hurt Eliza.

For now, Anna thought she would keep the information to herself. She would say nothing.

Eliza had encouraged her to keep searching the house to see if they could find more information about what they'd read, so she would say nothing until she had something more to say.

"There's always the attic," Eliza said to Anna. "That's one place we haven't been yet, and it has lots of things in there. There's sure to be something that will tell us more about this child mentioned in those documents."

Anna had been into the attic a few times, taking up old items that were no longer required in the house. It was dark and dusty, and as Eliza said, there were lots of things in there.

However, it wouldn't take just one visit to look through it all, and she wasn't sure how they could make continual trips up there without looking suspicious.

"There's a lot of things up there, Miss. It's not organised, and you'll get quite dirty," Anna warned.

Eliza brushed Anna's doubts aside.

"I know we'll find something up there," she said.

"Let's go up tomorrow night and then we can see what it's like and make a plan."

Anna nodded but still felt doubtful. She was impressed by Eliza's enthusiasm but wondered whether she was allowing it to cloud her judgement of the reality of the situation.

She was still curious about the documents and the child they spoke about, but the idea of going up into the attic reminded her of Lord Harrow's face when he'd seen her near his desk that day. Yes, he'd seemed angry, but when she looked back now, she wondered whether there was an element of fear. He knew about the hidden drawer in the desk and what was inside it.

Had it been more that he was concerned she might stumble across it? Considering these things made Anna wonder whether it was wise to continue, however interesting this mystery was.

But she found she couldn't deny Eliza's request and sighed inwardly, nodding in agreement that they would at least look at the attic before deciding what to do.

. . .

THE ATTIC WAS right at the top of the house, which meant that Eliza was less worried her father or any of the other servants might hear them. When they walked in, their skirts stirred up the dust lying on the floor, and both of them covered their mouths, coughing into their sleeves.

Anna held the lamp up high so they could look around the space before them.

Just as she remembered, there were things everywhere: pieces of furniture, trunks of items, with no organisation.

It wasn't even as if the furniture was all by the sides and the smaller items in front; everything was all over the place. She couldn't see how they would possibly be able to find anything amongst it all.

"WELL, there's a lot more up here than I thought," Anna said, and for the first time, Eliza started to hear some doubt in her voice.

IT MADE ANNA FEEL SAD, and against her better judgement, she found herself suggesting that it wasn't as bad as it looked. It definitely was, but she'd never seen the mistress look so alive since they'd started this adventure together.

Truthfully, Anna had enjoyed spending so much time with her. She'd always found her to be polite and kind, but as they'd spent time each day searching different parts of the townhouse, Anna had realised that she was so much more than that. She was surprised at how much they seemed to have in common, given their very different stations in life.

"IT'LL BE OKAY, Miss. We'll just start at one end and work our way through. We might not be able to come up every night, but I think—" She looked at Eliza and shrugged her shoulders, pleased to see the small smile return to her face.

"YOU'RE RIGHT, Anna. Of course we can do this," Eliza said with a look of determination on her face as she started looking through some of the items closest to where they stood.

"I THINK I FOUND SOMETHING," Anna called over to Eliza.

She stood looking at the basket on the floor. It had been hidden in the corner, but she had seen it through the spaces of the furniture in front of it.

After a few hours of sorting through furniture and some papers, she finally thought she might have found something that could be a clue to everything.

She climbed over to get a better look.

It was a baby basket, and there was a blanket inside—a pink blanket. As she stood there staring at it, she heard Eliza hurry over to where she was.

"That definitely looks like something," she said almost in a whisper.

But now that there was a clue that looked like it could lead them towards something, neither of them knew what to do.

"Pass it over to me, Anna," said Eliza.

Anna picked up the basket. It was clear that it was the kind of basket you would put a child in—a baby to sleep. The blanket was obviously one that you would swaddle that baby in before putting it into the basket.

She placed it on top of the set of drawers it had

been behind and climbed over to stand next to Eliza. Without thinking, she reached out and touched the blanket, feeling the softness of it between her fingertips. Her eyes widened at the thoughts that rushed through her mind, and she was suddenly overcome with emotion she didn't understand. She could feel her eyes start to tear up, and she blinked rapidly as she picked up the blanket and held it to her cheek.

Eliza didn't notice any of that because, once the blanket was out of the basket, she noticed a notebook that had been hidden underneath. She picked it up and opened it. It wasn't just a notebook; it was a diary. As she started to read the first page, it was clear that it was the diary of the mother to the baby they had read about.

CHAPTER 8

The two of them stood there, lost in their own thoughts—Eliza reading the diary, Anna with her face pressed into the blanket. Minutes passed, and then, as if mirroring each other, they looked up and at each other.

"It's a diary, Anna. I found a diary. It talks about the baby, a baby girl. It's a servant's diary. Her name's Mary. She talks about being in love—being in love with someone that she shouldn't be in love with, someone that couldn't possibly amount to anything. And yet, it says that not only was she in love with him, but that he was in love with her. It's got to be my father," she said, and she turned a few more pages, skimming through the words until she came across something that confirmed her suspicions. "It is. It's my father. It doesn't name him, but she calls him 'His Lordship.'"

Eliza's shoulders dropped. Just as before, when she discovered the documents in her father's desk, she couldn't decide whether the information was something she should know.

Sensing the change in her, Anna placed her arm around her shoulders, trying to offer some support.

In her other hand, she continued to hold the blanket tightly to herself. She didn't know why, but she felt an urge never to let it go.

"What else does it say?" she asked. "Does it say the baby's name?"

Eliza continued to skim through the pages of the diary, shaking her head.

"No, it doesn't. It doesn't say a name, just that it's a baby girl."

Then she looked up at Anna and realised what

the household servant was asking her. In the time they'd spent together, Eliza had shared the few memories that she still had of her mother, and Anna had told her that she remembered nothing about her own. She'd been just a baby when her mother had passed and knew nothing about her. It was clear that Anna was wondering about her own parentage, but a sudden suspicion came to Eliza's mind. She knew she needed to read the letters that were in her father's desk.

"No name is mentioned," she said again. "But now that we've found it, I'll take it to my room and read it properly. I'll let you know whatever I find out."

Anna nodded, and the two of them walked down the stairs and back into the main house. They parted ways, each going back to their own bedrooms, deep in thought.

It was only once she was inside her small room, with the door closed behind her, that Anna realised she still had the pink baby blanket in her hands. She held it to her face once again before folding it gently and putting it away in the back of the small cupboard that held her few clothes. Without knowing why, she knew that no one must know she had it.

ON HER WAY to her own room, Eliza passed her father's study, and for the first time since he'd gone out that night a few weeks ago, he wasn't in it.

The door was slightly ajar, and the room was dark.

She knew this would be her only opportunity.

She walked in as quietly as she could, reaching out her hand. She didn't want to have to use a lamp, so she did her best to feel her way around the furniture, eventually coming to the desk.

She tried to remember what Anna had done to trigger the hidden drawer. As she felt around, her hand came across a small button, which she pressed. The drawer popped out suddenly, and there lay the documents and letters exactly as she'd left them. She looked up towards the study door, aware of what she was doing, and before she thought about it too much and changed her mind, she picked up the pile of letters and pushed the drawer closed before making her way quietly out of the study again and continuing towards her bedroom.

. . .

Eliza placed the letters and the diary on her bed, then stood back, looking from one to the other. She didn't know which to read first, but she knew they were inextricably linked, especially once she realised that the handwriting on the letter envelopes was the same as the handwriting in the diary.

The letters were from Mary to her father.

While Eliza hadn't read the entire diary, the pages she had skimmed through towards the end spoke of heartbreak.

What had started as a love story full of joy and hope had ended very differently. She was frightened to read the contents of the letters. It was one thing to see the thoughts of another young woman in the pages of her diary, but she could only imagine what the letters to her father might say.

She took a deep breath and untied the string, taking the letters from the pile and placing them next to each other. She took them out of the envelopes and opened up the pages. They had been dated, so she put them in chronological order before picking them up, along with the diary, and taking them over to the small table by the window in her room. The lamp was already lit. As she sat down and started to read, she didn't realise how quickly the time had passed until she finished and looked out of her bedroom window to see the dawn starting to break.

EVERY SUSPICION she had was revealed to be true in the diary and the letters laid out on the table before her.

It was her father, her own father, who had sired an illegitimate child.

There had been a romance between himself and one of the house servants, a young woman named Mary.

It wasn't a one-sided love; it was clear from what Mary wrote in both her diary and in the letters that she sent to her father that it was a love reciprocated. It was hard to imagine her father being in love, and as she read about the moments they had shared that Mary described, it was even harder to imagine that the man she talked about was her own father, the man who always seemed so angry.

Mary spoke about a young man who smiled, who

recited poetry, who spoke of a future, one that he hoped they could find a way of sharing together. The young man that Mary described was unrecognisable to Eliza.

But it was obvious that the idealistic love that Mary and her father shared was never going to end well.

Mary had become pregnant and had been sent away.

In her letters, she pleaded for Eliza's father to come and see her. She didn't understand why they couldn't be together. He'd made promises, and she did her best to remind him of the future that he said could be theirs.

Each new letter seemed to suggest that Lord Harrow hadn't responded to the one before. Like in the diary, the first few letters sounded hopeful as Mary tried to persuade him that their love could overcome any obstacle. But her hopeful voice faded as it became obvious that her letters remained unanswered, and the last few were full of sadness and gentle reproach as Mary came to understand that the life she'd hoped to share with her love was never meant to be.

. . .

The last letter from Mary was the saddest of all, for wrapped up inside it was a note written by a different hand.

Mary had written to tell Eliza's father that their child had been born, a little girl, and that she hoped now she was here, he would come to see them both. There was a sadness in her words, but it was tinged with hope, as if she refused to believe that he would completely desert them.

The note with that last letter spoke about how just a few days after writing it, Mary had passed away.

The birth had been a difficult one, it said, and then finished with a reproach: "You broke her heart," it declared, "and so her body was too weak, too weak to be able to stay and bring up your daughter. This responsibility I now lay at your feet, your Lordship," it ended.

Eliza folded the letters back up, placed them back in their envelopes, tied the string around them, and set the small pile on top of the closed diary. She had seen the dates on the letters; they were from before she was born, and she was relieved to note they predated her parents' marriage. However, the thoughts she had been having since being in the attic began to coalesce in her mind. She knew she needed to speak to her father; she needed to hear the words from him and understand why he had behaved so terribly towards this young woman he had obviously loved.

For now, she put the diary and the letters in a drawer. Despite the dawn's arrival, she knew she needed to sleep before confronting her father. Her emotions were high, and if she spoke to him now, she feared the conversation would not go well, and she wouldn't get the answers she felt she deserved.

Just as she was about to get into bed, she heard a gentle knock on her door before it was opened, and Anna walked in.

"Morning, miss," she said, bobbing her head.

"I've not been very well this last night," Eliza said to Anna. "So I'm going back to bed. Could you please let Mrs Harris know?"

. . .

Eliza couldn't quite bring herself to look directly at Anna. She felt rather than saw the question on Anna's face as she backed out of the room and closed the door behind her.

More than ever, Eliza knew that she had to speak to her father. As she closed her eyes and sleep overtook her, she tried to make sense of everything she had read.

CHAPTER 9

The following day, Eliza's thoughts were still in turmoil. She'd spent most of the previous day in bed and had finally come down for supper, expecting to see her father at the table. However, it was another evening when he had gone out, and Eliza found herself eating her meal alone.

She hadn't planned to confront her father at the dinner table, but she had decided that after their plates had been cleared away, she would ask him if she could speak with him later on. Yet, that opportunity never arose. She heard him come into the house in the early hours, struggling to get to sleep that evening with every noise she heard, thinking that it might be her father coming home. She wondered if it was too late to go down and speak with him, but by the time he eventually came in, she knew she would have to wait until another day.

All of this was going through her mind as she walked through the day in what felt like a fog. She couldn't bring herself to speak to Anna until she'd spoken to her father, and so she spent the day avoiding her at any cost.

She could only imagine what Anna was thinking.

They had started to become so close, spending most of their days together when Anna wasn't busy with the tasks Mrs Harris, the housekeeper, had given her. Now Eliza knew that Anna must be wondering what had happened between them.

"I will definitely speak with him today," she thought. "This can't go on any longer."

Thankfully, as she walked down the hall and passed her father's library, she smelled the tobacco from his pipe and knew that he must be in the room.

She stuck her head through the doorway and saw him sitting in an armchair, his pipe in one hand and a glass of something in the other. She closed the door behind her and walked over to where he sat. He turned, startled.

"Eliza, what are you doing in here?" he asked, his tone suggesting he was always angry. She had become used to it and chose to ignore it.

"I need to speak to you about something, Father," she said, and without being invited, she sat in the armchair across from him.

The room's walls were covered in bookshelves, each one full. Her father liked reading, but she knew it was her mother who had been the avid reader. Because of that, he didn't come into the room that often, but now it was almost as if he was hiding. He looked at her with a frown, and Eliza knew that if she didn't speak quickly, she'd be told to get out in no uncertain terms.

"I know, Father," she said.

She saw a sudden flash of worry cross his face.

. . .

"You know nothing, Eliza," he said.

"Oh, but I do, and I have proof. I have proof of everything, so you may as well just tell me the truth. You've kept everything secret for so long, and it's not right. I should have known; I should have been told. You should have told me. Did Mother know?"

The words came tumbling out of her, and her father's mouth opened and closed as if he was trying to say something.

"Well, now's your chance. Now is your opportunity to tell me everything. It's time to explain yourself and your behaviour," she said finally.

She knew how rude and disrespectful she sounded, and at any other time, she would never have dared to speak to her father as she just had. But the anger and hurt that had been bubbling up inside her since she'd spent the night reading the diary and the letters she discovered suddenly came bursting out.

Her father looked defeated.

"I would have told you, Eliza. I would have had to eventually. Our life would have had to change, and so I couldn't have kept everything from you, not in the end."

For a moment, it was Eliza's turn to be confused. How would the revelation of an illegitimate child have changed their lives? she wondered.

Her father, noticing her confusion, stopped talking and watched her, waiting to see what she would say next. When she remained silent, he eventually spoke again.

"What are you talking about, Eliza?" he asked carefully. "What is it that you think you know?"

His voice sounded wary, but Eliza was so determined to confront him that she ignored it for the moment.

"Anna, of course, I know about Anna," she said bluntly.

Relief washed over her father's face until he realised what she had just said. Eliza was confused, not understanding his initial response, but as she watched the relief turning into sudden and deep shock, she forgot all about it.

"You... you know about Anna?" he said, his voice almost a whisper as he stumbled over the words. "What is it you know about Anna?" he asked her.

"Everything, Father. I know everything about her. I know everything about you and I know everything about her mother, Mary. I know that Anna is your daughter."

Her father sat back in the armchair with a thump, the colour draining from his face.

He put down the pipe and the glass, his hands shaking as if he thought he might drop and break them both.

Then, quite to Eliza's surprise, he put his head in his hands and shook it slowly from side to side. She didn't need him to say anything; everything that she'd read was confirmed in the response that she saw right in front of her eyes.

It was true. Anna was the illegitimate child they'd read about in the documents. Anna was her father's illegitimate child. Anna was his sister.

THE TRUTH of these revelations had circled in her mind since she'd read them, and while she had known them to be true, she needed to ask her father, to have him tell her the truth himself.

But no words were needed.

When he eventually took his hands from his face, he looked across at her, his eyes wide and his skin pale.

She expected him to say something, but he just sat there silently, his head continuing to slowly shake from side to side, almost as if he was trying to deny the truth that he had tried to hide for so long and was now being confronted with.

ELIZA FELT no sympathy towards him.

Perhaps that would come in time, but now she needed to understand how he could have made his daughter a servant, how he could have denied her existence, how he could have turned away from her mother, a woman he had purported to love.

. . .

"So, explain yourself, Father. I read everything, but I want you to tell me. I want you to help me understand how you could behave as you did."

Her father stopped shaking his head and took a deep breath, letting it out slowly.

"You must understand, Eliza. You know how things are. You know how our world works. How could I possibly marry a servant? How could that ever be a choice that I would be able to make? The idea that we could have been husband and wife, that we could have lived a life together, brought up a child together... it's so far from possible."

He spoke the words slowly, almost as if he was trying to convince himself as much as her.

For the first time, Eliza wondered whether they were even his words at all.

She'd never really known her grandparents, but they'd always seemed stern and aloof to her. Perhaps the decision had been taken out of his hands, but she wouldn't let him off the hook. If that was the case, then he needed to say those words to her himself. She sat and waited for him to continue.

He took another shaky breath, letting it out before once again saying,

"It just wasn't possible."

He closed his eyes, as if thinking back to the past, and when he eventually opened them again and looked at Eliza, it was as if a different man sat in the chair in front of her. Gone was the frown, the shocked look, and in its place, he looked sad.

"I loved her, you know," he said eventually. "I was young, and I thought my love for her would be enough. I thought it could be enough. I thought that love would be able to overcome our differences and that the world would accept us being together because of how much I loved her. But it was impossible. My parents, your grandparents, made it clear that it was impossible. And so what choice did I have? When I found that Mary had died, that there was a child, I tried to do the right thing. I thought that if she worked here, I'd be able to make sure that she was looked after, that she was educated. There was no way that she could ever know the truth, that anyone could. It would have been a terrible scandal, and it would have meant that when I eventually met your mother and fell in love with her, we wouldn't have been able to get married. How could we? And it was better for Anna to wonder about her parentage than know the truth, that she was illegitimate. That truth would have followed her around, caused her endless heartache, and ruined any chance for the future that she might have hoped for."

HER FATHER RUBBED his face with his hands.

"What would you have me do, Eliza?" he implored.

CHAPTER 10

Those words haunted Eliza now as she sat once more in the library, but this time on her own.

Her circumstances from the previous evening to where she found herself this morning now seemed unrecognizable.

Her father was gone.

She'd woken up, expecting to come downstairs, and stand by his side as he spoke to Anna and explained the truth of her parentage to her.

But now, that would never happen.

Eliza tried to think back to how her father had looked when she last saw him. She had no real experience in these things, but she'd noticed over the last few years that her father had started to drink more often, and she had begun to recognise the changes in his face that happened to a heavy drinker.

But it was the conversation she'd had with her father that weighed on her mind the most.

Was it that which caused the situation she now found herself in?

There was a light tapping on the library door.

"Miss?"

It was Anna, who stood in the doorway, looking at her and gave a small curtsy of respect.

"Can I get you anything, miss?"

Eliza sat unmoving, not knowing how to reply.

"My father... Could you get me my father?" she thought, aware of how ridiculous that sounded even to her own ears.

"A cup of tea, perhaps? You've not had your breakfast. Maybe something to eat? Shall I ask Mrs Jones to make you something?"

. . .

Eliza shook her head and forced a small smile.

"No, no, thank you, Anna," and then changed her mind. "Actually, a cup of tea would be nice."

Anna looked at her, searching her face before nodding and walking out of the door towards the kitchen.

"I don't know what to say to her," Anna said to Mrs Jones as she walked into the kitchen. "I know she wasn't close to her father, not as close as she used to be, but still, it must have come as quite a shock."

Mrs Jones nodded.

"Yes, it would have, and all we can do is just continue doing our jobs to the best of our ability. The young miss will need time, and while she's been running this house since her dear mother died, there's sure to be more for her to do since the passing of His Lordship."

. . .

His manservant had gone up to his lordship's bedroom that morning to open his curtains and help him get ready for the day.

But it wasn't a day that His Lordship would ever see.

He had passed away during the night, and it had been a shock to everybody.

Anna tried to push away any worries she had about her own future, instead concentrating on what she could do to help Eliza get through this terrible time. She wondered whether any of the other servants worried that they might find themselves jobless and homeless.

She knew that her worries weren't helped by the fact that she had nowhere to go. She had no home to return to, no parents who could take her in, no family of any sort.

Everyone she knew lived here under this roof, and she'd never been more starkly aware of that than at this moment.

"Come on, lass, whatever you're thinking, it will do you no good. There's still the house to run. Now, did Miss Eliza want something to eat?"

Anna's thoughts were dragged back from that

dark place by Mrs Jones' voice. The cook was right; there were still things to do, and she was worrying over a future that may never happen. Who was to say how things would turn out?

"No, nothing to eat, but she has asked for a cup of tea."

"Well then," said Mrs Jones, "let's get the tray ready. I'll put a couple of biscuits on there as well, just in case. It's not good for her to not have anything in her stomach at a time like this, and we need to get ready because there's sure to be some visitors. I'd like to think that some of His Lordship's acquaintances would come and pay their respects, and it won't be too long before his advisors arrive to speak to Miss Eliza. So, no more standing around; time to get busy."

Anna followed Mrs Jones' lead, getting the tea tray ready to take to Eliza.

. . .

When she put it on the small table next to where Eliza was sitting in the library, Eliza seemed to stare right through her.

"Thank you, Anna," she said.

Anna wanted to sit in the chair opposite her, to ask her if there was anything she could do.

She even considered wrapping her arms around the young girl, hugging her, trying to reassure her that everything would be alright.

But no matter how close they'd become over the last weeks, she knew that none of that was appropriate.

She was just a servant, after all, and no matter how well she and Eliza got on, Eliza was now the lady of the house. So Anna bobbed a curtsey, as she always did after pouring her a cup of tea, and left her sitting there.

There was no time to think about any of it once she was back in the kitchen.

Mrs Jones was keeping everybody busy. She'd done a bit of baking so that there was something to offer any visitors and had got down the best tea service they had.

One of the other young girls was washing everything up so it was clean and ready.

Mrs Harris was in the kitchen as well, and it was the first time that Anna had ever seen her out of sorts. She was wringing her hands gently as she walked around the kitchen, but she didn't say anything.

Anna had only ever known her giving orders constantly, and she found this quiet unsettling. But she wasn't given the opportunity to think much about that either as Mrs Jones gave her a list of things to do.

It was a little while later that she went back into the library to collect the tea tray. The cup of tea she'd poured for Eliza sat exactly where she'd left it, now cold, and Eliza looked as if she hadn't moved either. She sat upright, staring into the fire before her. She didn't even look at Anna as she came into the room.

"Shall I get you a fresh pot, miss?" Anna asked her.

. . .

ELIZA TURNED AT HER VOICE, blinking rapidly as if coming out of a dream.

"Oh, Anna," she said. "Did you pour my tea?"

"YES, miss. Quite a while ago, miss. It's cold now, though."

ELIZA LOOKED at the cup on the table.

"Oh," she said.

"IT'S OKAY, MISS," Anna said gently. "Shall I go and get a fresh pot made?"

ELIZA LOOKED UNCERTAIN, as if even such a simple request was too difficult for her to find an answer for.

"IT'S OKAY, MISS," Anna said. "I'll go and get a fresh pot. You stay here."

She picked up the tray and walked out of the room, knowing full well that Eliza wasn't going anywhere.

"I THINK the young miss is in shock," she said to Mrs Jones. "She's not touched her cup of tea. I'll make her a fresh pot and take it in, maybe stay with her while she drinks it."

"SHE NEEDS A SHOT OF BRANDY," Mrs Jones said, looking towards Mrs Harris, who nodded, realising that there was something she could do.

"I'LL COME BACK into the library with you," she said to Anna, "and I'll pour her a small brandy."

ONCE THE FRESH tea was made, the two of them walked towards the library together.

Anna had never spent time with Mrs Harris like this. It felt strange for them to be walking side by side and for the housekeeper not to be barking orders at her or telling her that whatever she was doing wasn't quite good enough.

Anna didn't imagine for a moment that this

would be a lasting change, but she was grateful for it nonetheless.

As she'd expected, Eliza was sitting exactly where she'd left her. The two women poured her drinks, Mrs Harris placing the glass of brandy in her hands.

"Drink this up, Miss Eliza," she said. "You've had a terrible shock."

Eliza lifted the glass to her lips and grimaced as she swallowed the burning liquid.

"Finish it up," Mrs Harris encouraged her, and she did.

The glass was taken from her hands and replaced by a cup of tea.

"Have a biscuit as well, miss," said Anna, and she watched over Eliza as she picked up the biscuit and nibbled at it half-heartedly before putting it back on the plate and taking a sip of tea.

· · ·

Mrs Harris nodded at Anna, encouraging her to stay in the library with Eliza, and then left.

Anna stood quietly nearby, watching as Eliza sipped her tea.

"I can't believe he's gone," Eliza said finally, turning to where Anna stood. "There was so much, so much that he needed to say, to do," she said, and then turned back to the fire.

Anna was confused by her words but stayed silent.

Eliza finished the tea and put the cup down just as there was a knock on the library door. Mrs Harris stood in the doorway.

"One of your father's advisors is here, miss. He needs to see you," she said. "Shall I bring him in?"

Anna watched as Eliza took a deep breath and let it out slowly. She stood up and turned to Mrs Harris.

. . .

"Yes, Mrs Harris, I'm ready. Bring him in."

"Go and fetch some fresh tea," Mrs Harris said to Anna, sounding a little bit more like her old self.

By the time Anna had brought another tray of tea into the library, Eliza and his lordship's advisor were already talking. They stopped as she came in, placed the tray down, and walked back out of the room. As the door clicked closed, she heard their voices start again, and she couldn't miss the worried tone in Eliza's as she responded to something the advisor had said to her.

CHAPTER 11

*E*liza needed to get out of the library.

She couldn't stand to be in that dark room any longer. She needed to be somewhere light and bright. She wanted to look out of a window and see other people. She wanted to be reassured that the world was still turning, that somewhere, normal life was still happening for someone. Her own life had been turned upside down in less than a day. It felt like everything she had known to be true was now in question.

HER FATHER HAD PASSED away after their conversation about Anna and his reassurance that he was going to tell her the truth about who she was.

Eliza had left him that evening still in the library.

She'd walked up to her bedroom, confused by the conflicting emotions she felt.

She loved her father, but she still couldn't quite believe he'd behaved the way he had.

She had heard his explanation, and yes, she understood it, but she didn't think that made it right. A young woman had been left to raise her child on her own, and his own daughter was a servant in his house, knowing nothing about her parents.

There was no way she could make that right in her own mind. But when her father had said that he would speak to Anna and tell her everything, she knew that that was at least a start.

BY THE NEXT MORNING, he was already gone.

He had died suddenly, the doctor told her without any real explanation, and Eliza assumed she would never really know what had happened.

It didn't matter now. It didn't matter why. She just felt the loss of him being gone, and the conflicting emotions she had had the night before were now compounded by a sense of guilt.

Perhaps she had had something to do with his

passing in some way. She shook the thought from her mind as she walked into the sitting room.

The curtains had been drawn, and now she walked over to the window and opened them, letting the light from the day come through into the room. She looked down on the street and watched people walking around, busy with their business. There were couples and groups; she could see servants walking quickly, almost at a run.

She took a deep breath. Yes, the world was still turning. She reassured herself that life still went on.

The conversation she'd had with her father's advisor came back to haunt her, and she turned and looked around the room. She had wondered why everything was starting to look shabby. She had wondered why things hadn't been replaced, why there had been no redecorating.

Everywhere looked now as it had back when her mother was alive. She wondered whether she had imagined that her father somehow couldn't bring himself to change it and wanted to keep everything as some kind of shrine to his wife.

But now Eliza knew the truth: there was no money.

There was no money to change anything, to replace anything, to fix anything, to redecorate anything. There was no money for anything.

Her father had made some bad investments, it seemed, and rather than just trying to recover from the loss, he tried to recoup the losses instead, but continued making one bad investment after another.

His advisor had tried to explain that he'd done his best to guide her father, but apparently, he wouldn't listen.

THAT WAS JUST LIKE HIM, Eliza thought.

She had assumed that he just never listened to her, but now it was becoming clear he didn't listen to anybody.

He had been determined to keep the house and as many servants as he could, and so, as well as there being no money, they were also in debt.

Eliza couldn't even begin to try to understand the extent of it all.

Her father's advisor had said that they would need to have a meeting about what the future may hold, but it wasn't something that Eliza could think about now.

He had hinted at selling the house, but Eliza had

balked at the idea. It was her home, and she couldn't imagine not living there.

"You'll be married one day," he had said to her, and she was reminded of Lord Whitfield. "Once you're married, you'll live in your husband's home. You won't need this one anymore. I suppose you could take a few of the things that mean the most to you," he continued, "but it would take the sale of almost everything to clear the debt."

Eliza had held up her hand and shook her head.
"I can't talk about this now, sir," she'd said to him. "I've just lost my father, please."

"Of course, miss," he said, "but we will need to have a conversation about it. Decisions will need to be made, and none of it can wait too long."

As soon as he'd left, she escaped the library, a room that she now associated with terrible news and confrontation.

As she looked around the sitting room, trying to block out the memory of that conversation, she saw Anna standing quietly in the doorway.

That was something else that she would have to think about and make a decision on.

She knew, while her father couldn't have the conversation with her, that Anna deserved to know the truth. But it was something else that she couldn't face today.

"Can I get you anything, miss?" Anna asked her, stepping into the room.

"No, thank you, Anna. I'm fine," Eliza said, and she turned back towards the window.

Anna stood for a moment watching her. There had been rumours about the conversation between her and her father's advisor, and Anna had found herself worrying again about what her future might hold.

When Eliza remained at the window, Anna made her way back to the kitchen.

Mrs. Harris had a list of things for her to do, and she spent the rest of the day busy at her work.

When she finally got to bed that night, she was exhausted. But just as she started to drift off to sleep, she thought again about the papers that she'd found in his lordship's desk and the mystery surrounding them.

She supposed that now she would never know anything more about the child they spoke about, and her days of wandering around the house with Miss Eliza, trying to find the answers, would be over.

CHAPTER 12

It was just a week after the funeral when her father's advisor stood once again in the library with Eliza, discussing what needed to happen to settle her father's debts.

"The house will need to go, the artwork will need to be sold, the furniture as well," he listed off emotionlessly.

Eliza couldn't help but wince as she thought about the destruction of her family home and everything she held dear. She knew, on one hand, that they were only things, only belongings, but they were also a link—a link to her father, to her mother, and to all that had gone before them.

The advisor made it sound so easy: "Just sell it all," was basically what he was telling her.

And then what? Rely on her husband for the rest of her life? She had hoped that perhaps the need to marry would have lessened with her father's passing, but instead, it was becoming obvious why he had arranged it in the first place.

But Eliza didn't like the idea of having to rely on Lord Whitfield.

While she was sure her father would have been happy for her future husband to help pay off his debts, that wasn't something she could bring herself to do.

She remembered the few meetings they had had.

He had seemed a gentleman, a kind man, and a man of honour.

He had spoken gently and respectfully of his late wife, and she had enjoyed watching his face light up as he spoke about his children.

Being able to share the loss of her own mother with him, and knowing that he understood how deeply we miss those we love no matter how long ago it was, was something she had appreciated.

There weren't many people she could speak to, and having found somebody, she didn't want to sully it with talk of money and debts.

. . .

But she would certainly need to be married and have a home to go to if her father's advisor had his way and sold everything out from underneath her.

"Surely there must be another way," she said. "Surely there's something that can be done where I don't have to lose my home and all my belongings."

"If there is," he said to her, "then I have yet to come across it. I have looked at all of your father's paperwork and I can't see another way. I'm open to suggestions, but really, if you're going to insist on trying to keep the house, then this would be a conversation best had with Lord Whitfield."

There it was, Eliza thought.

It didn't take long before she was no longer seen as a person in her own right but just as somebody's wife, unable to have thoughts and ideas of her own—they should be left for her husband, it would seem.

But she wasn't in the mood for an argument, so she let the words hang between them.

Her father's advisor cleared his throat.

"Well, when you can organise Lord Whitfield to come to the house and discuss all of this, then I shall meet with him," he said, before bidding her good day and leaving.

Not wanting to stay in the library any longer than she needed to, Eliza wasn't far behind him.

Without realising it, she found herself walking towards the kitchen. The house seemed so big and empty, and while she saw the servants busy at their work, it didn't stop the loneliness. As she walked through the kitchen door, the friendly chatter that she had heard stopped abruptly.

"Can I get you anything, Miss Eliza?" Mrs Jones, the cook, asked.

Eliza looked around at all the faces staring up at her, all of them surprised to see her in the kitchen. Her eyes settled on Anna's face, which smiled.

"Would you like to sit down with us, miss?" Anna asked.

There were a few short, sharp intakes of breath at

the question, but Eliza realised that she could think of nothing she would like more and nodded.

"Come on, everybody, move up," Anna said. "We can get another chair in here."

She organised everyone before placing a chair beside herself and encouraging Eliza to sit down.

Mrs Jones raised an eyebrow in Anna's direction but said nothing and passed a steaming cup of tea across the table.

Everyone sat silently, not knowing what to do or say, and it made Eliza wonder what they had been talking about before she interrupted them. She knew the gossip that had been going around the house.

She would have to have a conversation with Mrs Harris about everything, but she felt so confused about what the future might hold that she didn't know entirely what she was to say.

Prolonged silence, though, would only cause more gossip, she knew, and everyone would start to worry about what it all meant for them and their own security. Eliza wished she had an answer.

. . .

"Could I have one of those cakes?" she asked carefully, and Mrs Jones smiled and passed the plate across to her.

"Of course you can, miss."

Eliza was aware that she had barely eaten anything since her father had passed away, but sitting here amongst people who weren't asking her to sell her house and her belongings, who weren't confessing to deep dark secrets, who weren't pressuring her into a future she hadn't chosen for herself, she felt her stomach start to grumble and her appetite start to return.

As she finished the cake, the other servants at the table passed up plates of sandwiches and biscuits, and as she ate quietly and drank her tea, conversation started around her again—simple words of plans, of talking about family.

As Eliza listened, the worries that had been weighing heavily upon her started to slip away.

She realised that Anna had said nothing as she sat by her side, but she seemed to notice the weight of everything Eliza had been bearing dissipate as they sat at the table. Eliza turned to her and smiled, and Anna smiled back.

"Thank you, Anna," she said simply.

"This is your home too, miss, down here as much as up there. I know what it's like to feel alone," she said quietly, and Eliza nodded as she felt a single tear slip down her cheek.

It was the first since her father had died. There had been so much to get through—advisors, the funeral, keeping the house running. While she'd already done so much, she was surprised at how much more there was now that she was on her own.

Now, as she sat at this small, busy table, she realised that it wasn't just her own home she was fighting for, but also the homes of the people who worked for her.

They had worked for her father, and some of them for her mother.

This had become their home too, and she felt a renewed determination to keep it, not just for herself, but for them.

She looked around at each of their faces, smiled at Mrs Jones, and then back at Anna.

They weren't just servants; they were family. Eliza had always felt that way, and now, armed with the knowledge about Anna, it wasn't just a feeling, but a truth.

She needed to save the house for her, to preserve the belongings for her. Anna needed to know where she came from, and so much of that was here in this home that she'd always known but had never been aware of the significance.

Eliza squared her shoulders, thanked everyone for allowing her to join them, said good evening, and left.

She could only imagine the conversation once she left, and she found herself chuckling at the thought. It certainly wasn't the behaviour of a lady of the house, she thought.

CHAPTER 13

The conversation with Mrs. Harris had been short and to the point, while she tried not to give too much information away, mainly because she didn't want anyone thinking of her father.

However, she stated the facts: things were going to be tight.

Eliza was determined that no one would lose their job, and she was going to come up with a plan to ensure that was the case.

Until then, she said to Mrs. Harris, "Please make sure that the house is running as thriftily as possible."

. . .

Eliza knew that Mrs. Harris wasn't one to waste money, but she watched as the housekeeper's shoulders straightened with this new responsibility. She knew that thriftiness alone was not going to be enough; she had to come up with a plan to generate more income for the household. There were debts to pay as well as the running costs and wages of the staff. Eliza's mind ticked over, trying to think of ways to acquire the necessary finances.

She had asked for a list of her father's debtors from his advisor and decided that she would write to each one, explaining her situation and doing her best to reassure them that she would pay the debt in full, but asking for more time.

She hoped that correspondence from her own hand would be received better than something from her father's advisor, meaning they might take pity on her enough to agree to her terms.

Her father's advisor kept reminding her that she didn't know what she was doing, that she was out of her depth, and that these matters were best left to the men in her life.

If Lord Whitfield was unable to help her, then he

was there to step in instead. But Eliza was determined to handle it herself.

Each evening, she would sit in her father's study, writing down ideas, but she was yet to come up with one that would achieve what was required.

It was on one such evening that Anna came across her. The lamp lighting the desk was almost out of oil and quite dim.

The cup of tea that she'd brought in with her was cold and untouched.

The paper on the desk before her was practically blank.

She could feel the tears starting to well up in her eyes; they were tears of frustration and anger.

She felt so disappointed that her father had left her in this mess.

She hadn't heard the knock on the door, and it wasn't until Anna had called her name that she realized she was there in the room with her.

They had barely spent any time together since her father's passing. Eliza didn't know how to be with her, knowing all that she did, and she'd been thankful for how busy she had been, as it gave her the excuse she needed.

But now, the two of them in the room together, Eliza realized how much she'd missed her company.

They'd grown close, and for a time, she'd looked forward to the adventures they'd had together, hunting around the house for clues. It seemed a lifetime ago now.

"WHAT CAN I do to help, Miss Eliza?" Anna asked, but Eliza shook her head.

She'd started off so sure that she would be able to find a way through, but now she didn't think there was an answer other than either selling the house and all its belongings or agreeing to see Lord Whitfield.

He had tried to see her a few times; each time she'd refused, but he'd left her a small handwritten note with kind words of sympathy and understanding.

She was aware that other than selling the house, he was the only other hope she had of being able to pay off all the debt her father had accrued. He just seemed too kind for her to be able to do that to him.

. . .

"THERE MUST BE SOMETHING, Miss. There must be something that I can do, that we can do. Perhaps we could come up with a plan together."

Eliza wondered how much Mrs Harris had said to the servants; it seemed Anna knew the situation.

"I DON'T THINK there's anything to be done, Anna," Eliza finally admitted.

It was the first time she said the words out loud, and she felt disappointed in herself, feeling like she was giving up. But she didn't know what else there was to do.

"I DON'T BELIEVE THAT, Eliza. I don't believe that there's nothing, and I'm sure if the two of us sit and think about it, we can come up with something. We can work together, just like we did before. Look how close we got then. I know it could be the same with this too."

Eliza felt a slight guilt at Anna's words.

They hadn't come close; Eliza had solved the mystery.

It felt wrong to still not have explained it all to Anna, but now wasn't the time. There was hardly any point in explaining her parentage and that this was her real home if they were about to lose it.

"Pass me what you've written so far. Let me have a look at your ideas. I'll come up with some of my own," said Anna, "and then perhaps we can talk about it tomorrow. For now, Miss Eliza, it's late, you must be tired. The lamp is low, and it really is time that you went to bed and tried to get some sleep."

Eliza nodded in agreement.

She knew that Anna was right.

Waves of exhaustion had been washing over her all day, but she had tried her best to push through, thinking that if she just gave herself more time, the perfect idea would come to her. But it wasn't to be.

She got up from her chair and walked numbly out of the room, saying a quiet goodnight to Anna as she passed her, and then made her way upstairs to her bedroom.

Anna watched her go, her heart heavy. There had been a moment when Eliza had sat at the table in the kitchen with everyone, and Anna had seen a weight lift from her shoulders. She walked out that day focused and determined, but since then, Anna had seen all of that wear away, and the heavy weight of her father's death and all that it had left her with was now back.

Anna gathered Eliza's papers.

She wouldn't let her ideas come to nothing.

She knew how much this house and everything in it meant to her, and she would look through the plans she'd made so far and see what she could do to make them possible. She was sure that if they worked together, they could find a way.

When she'd mentioned them working together earlier, she thought Eliza might have said something about the mystery of the illegitimate child they discovered. She was sure that Eliza knew more than she was saying, but assumed that her mind was elsewhere.

Since her father's passing, she'd probably barely given it a second thought.

But the desire to know burned in Anna; she had so many questions. Perhaps one day, she thought to herself, and it reminded her of all the times that the cook, Mrs Jones, had said almost the same thing to her.

CHAPTER 14

Anna had spent most of the previous night looking over the notes that Eliza had written.

There were many good plans, but she couldn't see how any of them would be the answer to the financial trouble that she found herself in.

Anna had heard enough from different members of the household she worked alongside to know that Lord Harrow had left his daughter in a serious amount of debt. She didn't know the cause or the exact amount, but she knew that his lordship's advisors were doing their best to get Eliza to sell the house and everything within it.

The other servants believed this was necessary to

pay off his debts in full while still allowing her a small income of her own.

It seemed the selling of everything was required, and not just that, but if she was to have a life anything like the one she'd always known, she would need to marry Lord Whitfield.

So much was out of her control, and she had hoped that somebody new taking a fresh look over her ideas so far would have pinpointed the perfect one, the perfect idea that would have paid off the debts without having to sell the house and its contents, and without Eliza having to marry Lord Whitfield.

But even Anna could see that no idea like that existed.

ANNA WONDERED whether Eliza would be willing to part with some of the items in the house that had no real sentimental value, perhaps some of the belongings they'd stumbled across in the attic. She was ashamed to admit that that was really all she'd come up with, but she did feel that it was a start, and though it wasn't much, being able to start paying something back to her debtors was sure to relieve some of the pressure.

. . .

After breakfast, she went to find Eliza, who was once again sitting at the desk in her father's study.

The room her father had spent so much time in had now become like a self-imposed prison.

She gave the door a gentle knock and walked in. A good night's sleep, seemed to have done her some good. While Anna couldn't say that she looked too refreshed, she certainly looked more like herself.

"I read through everything that you've written," she said.

Eliza looked at her hopefully.

"I'm afraid I couldn't find anything amongst all your ideas that was a perfect solution," Anna said, "but I did wonder whether perhaps there was something in the attic that might be sold. They look like things from many, many years ago that have just been sitting up there forgotten. Perhaps they would fetch a decent price."

Eliza seemed to perk up.

"I hadn't even thought about any of those things,

Anna," she said, "but I think you're right. There's sure to be things up there that we can sell. If nobody has looked at them after all these years, then surely they wouldn't be missed." She smiled at her. "You were right, Anna," she said. "We do work well together. Perhaps Mrs Harris wouldn't mind making you available to me for the next few days, and we could go up and sort through some things together."

Anna was pleased to hear how positive Eliza sounded, and she was sure that Mrs Harris would agree to the request.

Over the next few days, the two young women spent almost every moment up in the attic, working their way through the many belongings that had been stored up there. They came across old paintings and pieces of furniture, neither of which Eliza recognised or remembered, and Anna was pleased to hear that she was happy to sell all of these things.

"If selling these things means that I get to keep those that are important to me, then so be it. I don't know who these people are, I don't know who used to use this furniture. Perhaps it was information that my mother would have shared, but it was nothing my father ever told me. It seems he was good at keeping secrets," she said.

Anna was reminded again of the secret of the illegitimate child but bit her tongue.

No matter how curious she was, she no longer felt it was her place to ask about something so intimate.

Once they'd made a pile of things for sale, Anna asked some of the male servants to carry everything downstairs.

Lord Harrow's advisor came to take a look, nodding in agreement that while nothing there would pay the debts off in full, it would be a good start.

Eliza was still waiting for some of the debtors to write back to her. The few that had so far had agreed to give her time; none of them had been clear on how much time, but she'd appreciated the sentiment.

She was drinking a cup of tea in the sitting room when a visitor was announced. It wasn't a name that she recognised, and when the older man was led into the room, he introduced himself as an acquaintance of one of the debtors that she'd written to.

"It seems the debt that your father owed has been passed to me. I understand you've asked for time," he said. "Well, I don't have time, so perhaps you just need to prioritise the debt that is owed to me." He looked around the room, frowning slightly. "If there isn't anything here that you can pay the debt with," he said, turning back to her and looking her up and down slowly, "perhaps we could come up with another arrangement."

Eliza could feel her cheeks start to redden.
Even though she was young and innocent in the ways of the world, she knew what he was suggesting.
"I have some things that I'll be selling," she said to him. "I'll make sure that you're paid."

He looked her up and down once more, more slowly this time.
"Well, if you don't manage it, then do remember my other offer."

Eliza rang the bell for one of the servants.

"Good day, sir," she said firmly and nodded to Anna as she walked in the door.

"Mr Percy is ready to leave now," she said, and before he could disagree, Anna led him out of the room and to the front door.

She walked back up to the sitting room and noticed Eliza's hand shaking.

"Is everything alright, miss?" she asked.

"We have to sell those items, and we have to get his debt paid first. The alternative he suggested—" she grimaced and shook her head. "Ghastly," she said.

Anna could only imagine.

She'd seen men like him before and knew the kind of payment they were always willing to take for any debt.

"Perhaps Lord Whitfield could help us find a buyer for the items," she suggested.

. . .

And though Eliza had longed to keep him out of the troubles she'd found herself in, she found herself nodding along.

While she was sure that her father's advisor would be able to sell the items, she was uncertain that he would ask for a fair price or that he wouldn't feel the need to take a fee of his own.

In the short time that she'd known Lord Whitfield, she knew him to be a man of honour, and she felt that that was exactly what she needed at this moment in time.

"You're right, Anna, he's just the man who will be able to help us. I know there are more things up in the attic that could be sold. Perhaps he'll be able to tell us which items would fetch the highest price. Maybe you could send one of the boys with a note to his home. Let me go and write one now—the sooner we start dealing with these debtors, the better," she said and grimaced once again at the memory of Mr Percy.

Anna nodded and waited for Eliza to come back. She hoped that Lord Whitfield was the man she imagined him to be and the man that Eliza imagined him to be as well.

. . .

When the boy came back, it was with a note from Lord Whitfield.

He was busy that day but suggested he come over the next afternoon.

Eliza sent the boy back with her reply, agreeing that that would be perfect.

She hadn't fully explained why she wanted to see him in her note; she felt it would be easier to discuss in person.

She was aware of the sensitivity of explaining why she wanted to sell the items in the first place. She felt embarrassed to admit it at all but hoped that he would be discreet with the information she shared.

That evening, as she ate supper, she thought again about their conversations. Her mind went back to how her father had made it clear she was to marry him.

Even now, she toyed with the idea—it would be the answer to so many of her problems. He would have a responsibility to pay off her debts once she became his wife, and she was sure she would find a way for him to do that and still keep her house.

. . .

SHE KNEW how much he had loved his late wife and how much he longed to keep her memory alive. If Eliza just told him that all she was trying to do was honour the memory of her own mother by keeping the house and the belongings in it, she was sure he would pay the debt her father owed, and she wouldn't need to sell the house or anything in it at all.

The thought of doing that had seemed wrong to her previously, but now she was starting to wonder whether it would be the answer to everything.

CHAPTER 15

The following afternoon arrived quicker than Eliza had imagined, and she was surprised to find herself looking forward to seeing Lord Whitfield again.

When one of the servants mentioned that she had a visitor, she assumed it was him. As she heard footsteps entering the room behind her, she turned around with a smile, only to be shocked to find Mr. Percy standing in front of her.

Eliza had thought that after the previous day, she wouldn't see him again. His suggestive words echoed in her mind, making her shudder slightly. As he walked over to where she stood, she felt a chill.

. . .

"It's good to see you again, Miss Eliza," he said. "I thought perhaps we could discuss more of how you were going to pay back this debt of your father's."

She tried to take a step back; he was far too close, closer than was proper. But she was standing in front of the table and couldn't move, and that seemed to please him more than she liked.

"I said that I would pay you back," she said, her voice a squeak.

She desperately hoped one of the servants would walk in.

"Oh, I know you did," he said. "But I thought we could agree on the terms."

He looked her up and down again as he had the day before, his eyes lingering on her neck and mouth.

. . .

"I don't know what you mean," she said. "I'll pay you back as soon as I've sold those items. You will get your money."

"I want to make sure I receive payment," he replied, leaning towards her.

He jumped back when footsteps and a loud clearing of the throat were heard.

He quickly moved away from Eliza, and she was relieved to see Lord Whitfield standing in the doorway, though surprised by the frown on his face. He couldn't possibly imagine the situation he had found them in was one she had agreed to.

The idea that he could think that of her made her feel uncomfortable. But why should she care what he thought? She gave her head a quick shake and started to walk towards him.

"Good afternoon, Lord Whitfield. It's good to see you."

. . .

Mr. Percy looked at Eliza, then at Lord Whitfield, and back at Eliza before smiling slightly towards her.

"I shall see you again, Miss Eliza," he said before nodding his head.

"Good afternoon, sir," he added and made his leave.

Lord Whitfield looked at Eliza once Mr. Percy had gone, unsure what to make of the situation he had walked in on. He had certainly heard stories about Mr. Percy and his personal dealings, especially with young women, and he was surprised to see him here with Eliza.

He hadn't imagined that she was that type of young woman.

Eliza stood there silently, then walked over to a chair and sat down, trying to gather herself.

"I can explain," she said. "It's not what you think." She tried to reassure him. "Please, Lord Whitfield, please come and sit down. There's so much I need to tell you."

. . .

Just as she was about to speak, there was a knock on the door.

"Shall I bring some tea, miss?" Anna asked.

"Yes, please, Anna," she replied.

She waited until the tea tray had been brought into the room. As Anna was walking out the door, Eliza asked her to close it behind her, ignoring the small frown on Anna's face as she nodded and did what was asked.

The conversation Eliza wanted to have with Lord Whitfield was not one she wanted the servants to overhear, especially not Anna.

She started by explaining Mr. Percy's presence that afternoon, then worked her way back, talking about the huge debts she had only been told about after her father passed away. Without knowing why, she told Lord Whitfield about the letters, the diary, and the documents she had found about her father's illegitimate child—Anna.

. . .

All the while she was talking, he refilled their cups with tea, listening intently. It wasn't until she finished that he nodded and finally spoke.

"It's been quite an eventful few weeks for you, Miss Eliza," he said. "I don't know how you've managed, but I'd like you to know you're not on your own now. I will help you in whatever way I can."

The relief Eliza felt was immense. The weight of all the knowledge she had been carrying alone began to lift, and she felt tears start to run down her cheeks. Lord Whitfield pulled out a handkerchief and handed it to her wordlessly. She dabbed the tears from her cheeks and eyes.

"Thank you so much, Lord Whitfield. It's such a relief to be able to speak to someone about everything. It's all been so much. Everything is such a mess."

. . .

"You know I can help you with your father's debtors," he said. "We can organise how to pay them."

"I found some things that I can sell, things that were in the attic. They don't mean anything to me; I don't know who they used to belong to. I've had some of the servants bring them downstairs. I just don't know how to sell them or where to begin," she said. "So any help would be greatly appreciated."

He nodded. It wasn't how he had intended to help her.

She must know that if they were to marry, he would pay off all her father's debts without having to sell anything.

But he wondered now, with her father no longer alive, whether she considered their marriage arrangement null and void. He didn't feel that this was the time to ask.

His heart had almost broken hearing everything she had gone through. He had heard rumours of her father's debts and poor investments, so the news hadn't really surprised him. But the extent of it all was quite a shock, and he hadn't realised Lord Harlow had allowed it to get so bad.

The news about Anna was unexpected as well.

He felt Eliza had taken the news better than the debts, but it must have still been a shock and changed how she saw her father. He just hoped it didn't change how she saw herself.

She sat there, so self-assured and, apart from the tears, composed. When he had first met her, all he could think was how young she was. But now he saw she was mature beyond her years, and he felt a growing respect for her. He couldn't imagine any other young woman handling everything she had told him as well as she seemed to be. Many others would have crumbled, but here she was, trying to find answers and a way to deal with it all.

"OF COURSE, I can help you with that, Miss Eliza," he said.

"THANK YOU, Lord Whitfield. Your help is very much appreciated. I just ask that you please say nothing about what I've told you regarding Anna. I know that I will need to tell her the truth. She deserves to know, and I feel such terrible guilt that I've said nothing so far. But I will find a time and a moment to share all of that information with her. So if you could please say nothing and allow me to do that, I'd be most grateful."

Again, Lord Whitfield was surprised by her maturity.

There was so much her father had left her to deal with; it just didn't seem fair. Yet, not once had she suggested that it was unfair. She had taken the responsibility on as her own.

Inside him, a spark of something he hadn't felt for a very long time warmed his heart.

CHAPTER 16

*A*nna poured the tea from the teapot into the two cups on the tray. The steam rose, and she felt it touch her cheeks gently as she bent over the small table.

Across the room, she could hear Lord Whitfield and Eliza talking softly with each other. Every now and then, she would hear one of them laugh.

Once she had finished pouring the tea, she looked up and across to where they sat, thinking about how close they had become.

She remembered the anxious fear Eliza had felt about meeting an old man she had never known.

The idea that her father had arranged for her to marry a friend of his had filled her with dread.

Even after that first meeting, her opinion of him had started to change.

Now, as Anna watched the two of them together, she wondered how Eliza might feel about Lord Whitfield.

She had found him to be nothing other than a man of honour. He had always been respectful to her and kind. He had never spoken down to her, even though she was a servant, unlike so many men of his standing. Even men who weren't of his standing, she thought, made themselves feel better by looking down on those less fortunate than themselves.

But not Lord Whitfield. If anything, he always seemed to treat her with care.

As far as she was aware, there had been no sign of Mr Percy since Lord Whitfield had come along to support and help Miss Eliza.

That terrible man was long gone, or at least it seemed, and for that, almost more than anything, she was grateful. The couple of times she had seen him here, she wasn't sure what his intentions with Eliza were, and it concerned her that there would be nobody to step in to protect her. But now that Lord

Whitfield was here, Anna knew that she didn't have to worry about that anymore.

She smiled again as she heard Eliza's laugh at something Lord Whitfield had said before leaving the room to attend to the many other things she had to do.

Eliza watched as Anna left and wondered again how she might tell her the truth about everything she had found out.

Lord Whitfield noticed the small frown on her face.

"The time will come, Eliza," he said. "The time will come, and I will help you. But for now, there are so many other things that need to be done to make sure that your place, that everyone's place, here in this house is secure."

Eliza looked up at him and smiled. She knew that he was right.

She would have been lost without him over these past few days. It seemed that he knew exactly what to do.

He'd helped to find an auction house to take the items she had decided to sell. He'd made sure that she got a good price. He'd stayed by her side, explaining carefully that it would be easy for a young woman to be taken advantage of, for the men here to suggest that the art she had for sale wasn't worth as much as he knew they were.

Having seen the auction houses, she could understand what he meant. They weren't a place for a woman, and she was grateful to have him there with her. Over time, she felt her confidence grow.

It wasn't just his help with practical things that she found herself enjoying; the more time they spent together, the more personal information they shared with each other. She found him the easiest man to talk to that she had ever known.

Whenever he eventually had to leave, she was left with a sinking feeling of disappointment.

"Thank you," she said to him. "And I don't just mean about that, but thank you for everything. I don't know how I would have managed without you, without your help."

Eliza could feel her cheeks start to redden as she blushed. She hadn't meant to make her thanks sound so personal, and now she was concerned it would be awkward between them. But he smiled gently, his eyes lighting up at her words.

. . .

"I believe, Miss Eliza, that you would have managed perfectly well without me, but it has been a great honour to help you during such a terrible time."

He bowed slightly and then laughed, which helped to lighten the mood.

Eliza had been surprised by his sense of humour; her father had always been so stern.

She wondered whether it was just that he was constantly worried. There was a lot he had been keeping to himself over the years, Anna's existence as well as all the debts he had got himself into. All of that must have weighed on his mind.

She couldn't say that she understood his behaviour entirely, but she found, now a few months on from his passing, that she was trying to.

Lord Whitfield had helped her try to understand that her father was just a man trying to do his best.

"It's all we can do."

She could understand that point of view, but it still didn't make his behaviour right in her eyes. Even if she did come to a place of forgiveness, she didn't think she'd ever truly understand everything he had done.

. . .

But she pushed it all from her mind. There was enough for her to focus on in the here and now, more important things, dealing with people who were still here. How she felt about her father could wait, she decided.

When Whitfield had to go, Eliza felt the same sinking feeling that was becoming familiar to her.

When she first felt it, she assumed it was loneliness at his leaving, knowing she would now be in the house on her own, albeit with the servants, but that was different. She had felt lonely when her father was alive; she knew what that felt like, and this wasn't that feeling at all.

Their relationship had eased into friendship very quickly, but now Eliza knew it was deepening into something else. She couldn't deny the way her heart beat faster when he entered the room or the way her breath caught in her throat when he smiled at her.

Every now and then she would think about the marriage arrangement that had been organised between him and her father. She had not mentioned it to him, and he had said nothing either.

She wondered what he thought. Perhaps he was being helpful because he thought he had to.

Perhaps he was grateful that now her father had died, it meant he probably didn't have to marry her.

All of these thoughts were confusing on top of everything else, but she found herself hoping that the reason he was helping her was because he enjoyed her company too. She had no experience of men, but she couldn't believe that the smile and the kind words he always had for her weren't genuine.

As Eliza lay in bed later that night, she thought again about Lord Whitfield.

She had eaten her supper that evening on her own, and while there were always servants somewhere around the house, she started to think about how it might be if she were to marry.

She knew that Lord Whitfield had children, and the thought of childish laughter throughout the house made her smile and lifted her spirits. She hoped that Lord Whitfield might bring up their previous marriage arrangement in conversation one day.

When he had first been mentioned to her, she shied away from the idea. He was a man she didn't know, a man who was friends with her father. But now that she did know him, she saw him in a very different light.

He wasn't just an older man or simply a friend of her father. He was kind and caring, supportive while also being funny and interesting. He wanted to hear what she had to say, and she found that when she was with him, she felt capable of almost anything.

As she drifted off to sleep, she knew that he was exactly the kind of man she would want to be married to.

CHAPTER 17

*E*liza had just got home from spending the afternoon with Lord Whitfield and his two young children. It was the first time she had met them, and she felt that she'd fallen in love with them both at first sight.

They were funny like their father, intelligent and kind, and they welcomed her in a way she could never have imagined doing when she was their age.

Her father had never suggested that he would marry again after her mother died, but even if he had, Eliza wasn't sure she would have been as accepting of another woman in her life as Lord Whitfield's children seemed to be.

She smiled as she remembered the games they

played together, especially that last walk around his beautiful garden.

The children had run around the hedges and rose bushes, chasing each other and giggling. Every now and then, Lord Whitfield would chase them too, but mostly the children played while the adults walked. It was everything she imagined married life with children would be.

She had been surprised by his invitation and hoped it meant his feelings for her were changing into something more. He had asked if she would like to come again, and she agreed without hesitation.

Now that she was back home, it felt so empty.

She walked up to her mother's bedroom, opening the door and going inside. It had been kept exactly as her mother had left it; it was cleaned regularly and always smelled of her favourite fragrance. Eliza hadn't come up here for a long time, but now she sat on the bed and tried to reach back to the few memories she still had of her mother while she was alive.

The strongest one was of her laughing.

She always remembered her mother being full of joy and happiness, and she always managed to make others around her feel the same. "I wish you were here, Mother," she thought as she ran her hand across the bed covers.

She took a deep breath, got up, and walked out of the room, closing the door softly behind her.

The next few weeks were filled with visits to Lord Whitfield's home.

She spent time with his children and even invited them all to come and spend time with her at the townhouse.

She loved how the house sounded filled with the laughter of children.

Lord Whitfield continued to help her make sense of her father's business dealings, helping to pay off the most pressing debtors.

She hadn't seen Mr Percy for weeks and hoped that now she'd finally paid everything her father owed him, she wouldn't see him again. She was surprised that his visits had stopped and wondered whether Lord Whitfield had spoken to him. If so, it was yet more proof that he was someone she could rely on.

. . .

She'd been so busy with everything that she'd barely had a moment to think about Anna. Of course, she'd seen her in passing, but the close conversations they'd had seemed a distant memory.

She knew it was partly because she was keeping her distance. She knew that if she spent too much time with Anna, she would blurt out the truth of her parentage, and she felt unsure about how to handle all of it.

On one hand, she knew Anna deserved to know the truth, but the more she thought about what the truth was, the more concerned she was that knowing it would just cause pain and heartache.

At the moment, Anna knew nothing about her father, only that her mother had died when she was very young. To know that her mother had died of heartbreak due to being abandoned by Anna's father, the man she loved—perhaps that truth would be too much.

She had spoken to Lord Whitfield about it a few times, but she was still no clearer on what the right thing to do was.

A few weeks later, when she was visiting Lord Whitfield at his home, she almost brought it up with him again, but he seemed to brush her concerns aside and instead invited her out to the garden.

The children had been put to bed by then, and it was now just the two of them. As he guided her out to the garden, lanterns had been set up, the lights glowed beautifully, casting shadows and making everything feel a bit like a fairy tale.

Eliza's breath caught at the beauty of it all, and she turned to see Lord Whitfield looking at her, his eyes soft and warm, an expression she had seen a few times but only now understood its meaning.

"I KNOW your father arranged for a marriage between us, Eliza, and I know how strange and forced that must have seemed. But I would like to think that this time we've spent together has helped you see that my feelings for you are true. While at first, I was looking for a mother for my children, I know now that in you, I've not only found that but also a woman who could be a wife for my heart."

ELIZA FELT tears well in her eyes at the beauty of his words. She realised this was all she'd hoped for, and as he reached across to take her hands in his, her heartbeat quickened.

"Would you do me the honour of becoming my wife?" he asked, and when she nodded before she could speak, he pulled her into his arms and kissed her.

When he pulled away, Eliza was breathless.

"Oh, Lord Whitfield," she said, and he laughed.

"You should call me Thomas now," he said.

"Thomas," she said, enjoying the way the name sounded as she spoke it. "I had so hoped that it wasn't just me who felt this wonderful thing growing between us. I can't think of a man I would rather be a wife to than you."

Suddenly, she thought about his children and what they might think, but as if he could read her mind, he reassured her.

"They know. I asked them first, and they were so

excited at the idea that you would be their new mother."

Eliza felt like her heart was fit to burst. As the two of them walked around the beautiful gardens, enjoying the evening, it was only the small niggle of Anna in her thoughts that kept it from being perfect.

CHAPTER 18

*E*liza stood with Lord Whitfield, smiling at the servants of her household.

They had just announced their engagement, and she was pleased to see how happy everyone seemed.

It made such a change from how the previous months had been. She recognised the strain that everyone had been under, wondering what their future held, but now they knew it was secure.

Lord Whitfield had spoken to her about the remaining debts in her father's name, and he had made it clear that she didn't need to sell anything else to raise the money to pay them off. As far as he was concerned, now that they were going to be husband and wife, the responsibility of paying those debts was his.

Eliza had wanted to refute that, saying that it was her responsibility and that it wasn't fair on him to have to do that for her.

"I don't feel that I have to do anything, Eliza," he reassured her. "It's an honour to be able to help you, just as it was previously by helping you to sell those things at auction with you. But now, let me do this. Your household deserves to feel safe, knowing that they won't lose their home or their livelihood."

She nodded at his words, realising that it was the right thing to do for them and that it was just pride that was causing her to feel that she needed to pay the debts off herself.

"Alright," she said, and then smiled. "But for that reason alone, I don't want you to ever think that I've married you so that I don't have to pay these debts myself."

. . .

He smiled at her, love sparkling in his eyes as he bent down, bringing her hand up to kiss it.

"I would never think that," he said.

They had both spoken to his children and the rest of his household, and now, as they stood there together, having shared the news with hers, she started to feel the excitement bubble up inside her about what the future might hold.

Anna came up to her afterwards, congratulating her personally, and Eliza was reminded once again that she needed to speak with her.

After his proposal, she had sat down and spoken to Lord Whitfield about her concerns regarding telling Anna the truth, but he believed that Anna was strong enough to deal with the knowledge.

"From what I've seen of Anna," he said to her, "she is a strong and capable young woman. I think she deserves to know the truth. Ultimately, it's your decision, Eliza, and I'll support you whatever you decide, but perhaps we should try to think about how we might feel not knowing where we've come from, especially if it were to come out at some point in the future that we could have been told that information."

Eliza knew that he was right, and thanking him for his wisdom, she knew that the next decision was deciding when to speak to Anna about everything that she had found out.

Anna was so pleased that Eliza had found happiness with Lord Whitfield. She'd seen from the very beginning what a good man he was and, watching as they grew closer, she felt happy knowing that Eliza wouldn't be alone.

She was even more pleased that Eliza had asked her to help organise the wedding celebrations. It had seemed such a long time since they had spent time together, and Anna looked forward to this opportunity.

Eliza had asked Anna to meet her in the drawing room that afternoon. It wasn't a room that was used very often, and as Anna made her way there, she wondered why Eliza wanted to see her here rather than the usual sitting room she liked to spend time in.

The drawing room was quiet and out of the way of the hustle and bustle of the household servants. Perhaps she just doesn't want to be disturbed, she thought.

She walked into the room, and Eliza was already there waiting for her. There was a tea tray on the table; it was a familiar sight. Eliza always liked a tray of tea to be available, and Anna was slightly surprised to see her pour her a cup as she invited her sister to sit down on the chair opposite.

"Do you have plans for the wedding celebrations?" Anna asked Eliza.

"Yes," Eliza said vaguely and nodded. "And we will discuss those plans, Anna, but there is something else that I need to speak to you about. There's a different reason I asked you to meet me here in this room. There's something that I need to tell you."

. . .

"Is everything alright?" Anna asked.

Eliza's tone worried her.

"Yes, I'm fine," Eliza said, forcing a smile. "This isn't about me, Anna. This is about you."

Anna started to feel a sinking in her stomach. Was she going to be asked to leave? Had she done something wrong? Thoughts of her future and what it might mean if she wasn't part of this household suddenly seemed dark and unknown.

Eliza reached across, taking Anna's hand in hers.

"I should have told you this as soon as I found out, but I didn't know how to. And then everything with my father..." Her words hung in the air between them.

Anna felt confused and waited for Eliza to explain.

"It's about your parentage, Anna," she said simply.

Now Anna felt a real sense of concern.

For so many years, she had wanted to know any information she could about her mother and possibly her father, but now that it seemed she was about to find out, she was frightened about what she might learn.

Eliza took a deep breath, letting it out slowly. "The illegitimate child that we found out about, Anna, the one that my father hid the information about... it's you."

Anna felt stung by the words, not understanding the enormity of what she had been told.

She was Lord Harrow's illegitimate child. She couldn't quite make sense of it in her mind.

"I... I don't understand," she said.

"It's you, and you are my father's daughter," Eliza repeated.

And then, before she lost her courage, she told Anna everything that she'd found out.

She talked about the diary and everything that she'd read in it and how it made sense of the documents that they'd found.

She spoke about the letters that she'd read from Anna's mother, Mary, to her father. And then, last of all, she told Anna about the conversation that she'd had with her father the night before he passed away.

"He had admitted to everything," she finished, "and he had said that he was going to tell you the truth himself, but of course, that became impossible. And then I didn't know what to do. I'm very sorry that I've kept it from you up until now."

Anna felt a deep sense of shock.

In many ways, it all made sense; in others, it felt so unreal she couldn't quite grapple with it. She felt a mix of emotions.

She was grateful that Eliza had told her, but she felt betrayed that the secret had been withheld from her for so long. She felt sadness for her mother and anger towards Lord Harrow.

She couldn't yet think of him as her father because how could a father behave in the way that he had? She tried to understand, but it was too soon.

. . .

"THANK you for telling me the truth, Eliza. I appreciate it. I hope you understand that I need some time to make sense of it all."

"OF COURSE, Anna. Of course, I understand," Eliza replied and then watched as Anna stood up, placing her cup of tea that had remained untouched back onto the tray and walking out of the room as if in a daze.

ANNA WALKED out of the room, unaware that Eliza was watching her.

She felt numb; there were so many emotions coursing through her, so many thoughts racing through her mind that she didn't know where to begin.

She knew that if it had been anyone other than Eliza who had told her, she wouldn't have believed it. But she knew that it had to be the truth. She didn't know what any of it meant for her future. For the moment, she was struggling to reconcile everything she'd learned with her past.

. . .

She'd been a servant in the house of her father all this time, calling Lord Harrow 'father' felt strange, but apparently, it was the truth.

She would like to read the documents, the diary, and the letters herself, but for now, she made her way upstairs to her bedroom. There were things to do, chores to finish, a wedding to plan, but Anna wasn't sure that she could face any of that, not right now. For now, she just needed to be on her own.

She sat down on her bed, looking around at her small room, the only place of her own that she'd ever known. Still unable to make sense of everything she had just found out about herself, she lay down on her bed fully clothed and squeezed her eyes shut as the tears started to roll down her cheeks.

CHAPTER 19

Now it was Anna who did her best to avoid seeing Eliza.

While she appreciated knowing the truth, she was still unable to reconcile her feelings about it.

On the one occasion that she'd seen Eliza since finding out the truth, she'd been reassured of the young woman's support. Eliza told her that she understood the difficulty and hoped that Anna would allow them to face it together. Anna had nodded; all of Eliza's words made sense, and she'd seen the hurt in her face at Anna's distance. But she still needed time.

. . .

OVER THE NEXT FEW WEEKS, Anna found herself thinking about her childhood here in the townhouse.

She tried to recall memories of Lord Harrow and any interactions she'd had with him. She was aware that he had ensured she would be educated, that at the very least she could read and write.

She tried to see that as something a father might do for his daughter. She knew that in a way, he was the man who had raised her.

While she had been looked after by the other servants in the house, especially Mrs Jones, the cook, her father figure had been Lord Harrow.

She'd never really recognised it before, never thought of it that way, but as she thought back to the years when she was a child, she knew it to be true.

She wondered if it was his way of trying to make amends for how he had treated her mother. She wondered whether he had any feelings towards her as his child. Had he ever thought of her that way? She supposed now that she would never know.

She still felt betrayed, but she was starting to remember the deep respect she had always felt for Lord Harrow. She wondered now whether those feelings were similar to a kind of love, the love one would have for their father.

. . .

Eventually, she knew that the only person she could speak about it with, to try to make sense of it all, was Eliza. One afternoon, that's exactly what she did. Eliza brought the diary and the letters, and they went into Lord Harrow's study. Anna went up to the desk, triggered the secret drawer, and took out the documents. Then the two of them laid everything out and sat down to look at it all.

"You should read it all, Anna. It's your past, and while it doesn't explain everything, it will tell you a lot, far more than what I have been able to say. Perhaps it will allow you to make more sense of it all," Eliza said, getting up to leave, thinking that Anna would prefer privacy.

But she stopped when she felt Anna's hand on her wrist.

"No, Eliza, please stay," Anna said to her.

. . .

The two young women sat in silence as Anna took her time reading everything before her. When she'd finished, she sat back, tears running down her cheeks. Eliza passed her a handkerchief, and when it seemed like the tears would never stop, she reached across and gently wrapped her arms around Anna, her sister.

After a few moments, Anna pulled away.

The story she had just read was heartbreaking, and she still didn't fully understand all of it. She longed for Lord Harrow to be here so she could question him, and she wondered what he had intended to tell her before he passed away.

There were still gaps, and while reading it had answered some questions, in many ways, it had created so many more.

She was still unsure how she felt about Eliza.

It felt strange to think that they were sisters, and yet she had waited on her, served her. While she knew that Eliza hadn't known the truth until recently, it still felt uncomfortable to think about how different their childhoods had been.

. . .

"I don't know what to think," Anna said. "I don't know what to feel."

She could feel Eliza's eyes on her, as if she expected Anna to suddenly have made peace with it all. Anna knew that would take time.

She looked up at Eliza. "It's so strange to think that we grew up in this house, both of us together and yet so different."

Eliza nodded, understanding exactly what she meant.

"I would have loved to know that I had a sister," she said to Anna.

She spoke about the loneliness she had often felt, especially since her mother had died. She talked about her childhood experience of living in the townhouse with her mother and father, and eventually just her father.

She encouraged Anna to share her memories too.

In some ways, there were similarities, especially when they were very young, but their lives had changed once Anna was old enough to go into service. It was something that Eliza could never make right; she could never change the past.

"I'm sorry for all of that," she said to Anna. "But I promise that the future will be different, your future will be different, and I hope that you can trust me to make sure that happens." Anna nodded, knowing that it would take time, but feeling hopeful.

"I need to know more," she said. "I need to know more about my mother, if it's possible."

"I'll help you in any way I can," Eliza reassured her.
The two of them parted ways, still unsure what it meant for each of them.

Anna sat in her room, looking over the diary, letters, and documents she had taken from Lord Harrow's study. Eliza had reassured her that these were hers now—they were about her past and her family, and she should have them.

As Anna read over them again and again, she started to feel closer to her mother.

In some ways, she started to feel like she understood Lord Harrow, her father, more.

Reading about the hopes and dreams her mother had shared helped her realise that at some point, there had been a deep love between her parents. She could understand more about herself as she understood more about them.

While her relationship with Eliza felt raw and new, the young woman was doing her best to put things right. But Anna was still surprised when Eliza asked to speak to her and explained that, as the eldest child, the manor was rightfully hers.

"But I'm illegitimate," Anna reminded her.

Eliza waved it away. "To me, that's irrelevant," she said. "It's your birthright and the right thing. Besides, I will have my own household soon enough, and I need to know, as my sister, that you will be well provided for."

. . .

"I don't know the first thing about running a house," Anna said.

"Neither did I," Eliza reminded her. "But if I can learn, then you can too. And I will be here with you, helping you and supporting you."

It felt like yet another thing that Anna had to try to come to terms with, but she couldn't deny that she felt excited at the prospect of having a house of her own.

"I will speak to Mrs Harris, the housekeeper," Eliza said.

At the mention of her name, Anna's stomach dropped. She remembered the harshness she'd always encountered from the older woman and wondered how this difference in their roles might change her behaviour too.

. . .

"She's never liked me," Anna said to Eliza. "Mrs Harris has never liked me. I don't think she's going to take the news very well."

"It doesn't matter how she takes the news," Eliza said. "It's the truth, and she will have to get used to it, just like everybody else in the household. And dear sister," she said, smiling, "so will you. We all have new roles now, but we will work together, you and I, and we will make this townhouse a wonderful place once again."

Anna smiled and nodded, remembering how things had been before Lady Harrow had died. There had been joy in the house then, but after her death, as the years went on, that joy had seemed to fade. The idea that the house could be full of joy again filled her with hope for her future.

She hadn't missed the fact that Eliza had called her 'sister', and she knew that even though there were still many feelings to work through, having a sister made her happy too. She suddenly felt less alone than she ever had before. She had always known she could rely on Mrs Jones, but having Eliza by her side filled her with confidence for what she was now being asked to do.

CHAPTER 20

Anna could feel the eyes of the other servants upon her as she walked down the hallway. She knew that Eliza had had a conversation with Mrs Harris and imagined that Mrs Harris had now spoken to everybody else. The gossip mill would be going mad, she thought.

Eliza had told her that the conversation with Mrs Harris had gone well.

"I just told her the truth," Eliza said. "I told her everything and explained that you are my father's oldest child and so it's right for you to run the townhouse now that he has passed away."

. . .

Anna didn't believe for a moment that it had gone as smoothly as Eliza thought.

Perhaps Mrs Harris had taken it well during that conversation, but Anna didn't doubt for a moment that she would have something to say about it behind her back. Thankfully, Anna heard nothing, so whatever gossip was happening, everyone was at least keeping it out of her earshot.

"I appreciate that Mrs Harris knows everything," Anna had said to Eliza, "but I would still feel better if we worked together until I was clear on everything that I have to do."

"Of course," Eliza replied.

In Anna's mind, that meant until Eliza got married and left to go and live with Lord Whitfield.

She knew that she certainly wouldn't feel comfortable running the household while Eliza was still there. But also, her hope was that everybody would have got used to her being in charge by the time Eliza left.

. . .

Most days, Anna woke up feeling full of nerves, and they only dissipated once she was with Eliza.

As they walked around the house, Eliza explained everything that needed to be done.

Anna found that there were many things she already knew about. It was surprising how much you learned about what needed to be done to run a house when you were a servant, mainly because you were doing all the jobs, she thought to herself, trying not to feel bitter.

Her relationship with Eliza was less strained than it had been, and Anna found that the more time they spent together, the less strained it became.

It was almost as close as it had been when they'd first started the adventure that led to where they were today.

She remembered those days, thinking about how much she had longed to find out the truth. While she was adjusting to it now, there had been a period of time when she'd wondered whether finding out the truth was really the best thing at all.

. . .

ANNA HEARD footsteps coming towards her and saw Mrs Harris as she turned the corner, walking in her direction.

"GOOD MORNING, MISS," Mrs Harris said.

IT ALWAYS TOOK Anna by surprise when Mrs Harris called her that. When she'd done it at first, Anna thought she was being sarcastic and trying to be disrespectful, but the more she did it, the more Anna realised that wasn't the case.

She'd been quite surprised at how helpful Mrs Harris had been and wondered whether she'd been unfair in thinking Mrs Harris hadn't taken the news of her birthright well when Eliza told her about it.

ANNA KNEW that wasn't the case with some of the other servants.

Many of the younger girls struggled to understand Anna's new role and the change it meant for their relationships. While she'd never had any real close friendships, they had been friendly. There had been times of laughter and sharing, and almost every evening they'd all gathered around the table in the kitchen to share their meal. Those had been times of stories of the day, but that had all changed now.

Many of them struggled to know how to see her as the lady of the house.

It didn't help that there had been a few errors she'd made, misjudgements of what the house needed. She hadn't been on top of certain orders, and there had been meals that Mrs Jones hadn't been able to make in full. Those gaps in her knowledge made her feel insecure that she would ever be able to manage on her own.

Mrs Harris stopped in front of Anna and, after having greeted her, asked if now was a good time for them to discuss the plans for the week. Anna knew that would involve any visitors, what meals needed to be prepared, any cleaning and organising, and there would also be some discussion over the plans for Eliza's future wedding.

Standing there on her own, Anna felt out of her depth and knew that her eyes were searching for Eliza, hoping that her sister would suddenly appear to be able to help her.

. . .

"I can help you, Anna," Mrs Harris said gently, and Anna was surprised to see a smile on the older woman's face.

It was the first she could ever remember receiving from her.

In many ways, the change in Mrs Harris's behaviour towards her was the most confusing. She could understand the difficulties between her and the servants she used to work alongside, but Mrs Harris's seemingly instant acceptance of her new role and position in the house was something she didn't quite understand. She brushed the thoughts away.

"Thank you, Mrs Harris. I'd appreciate that," and she smiled back.

They walked towards the study, and Anna knew that while it had always been Lord Harrow's workspace, it was now hers.

Eliza had mentioned a few times that she should feel free to redecorate however she chose, but having no experience of any such thing, Anna wouldn't know where to start. She decided that for now, she would leave everything as it was.

It meant that as she walked into the room with Mrs Harris behind her, she felt like an interloper. But it also brought back memories of the man she eventually discovered was her father.

She remembered all the times she'd seen him working in here, but her greatest memory was of the last time she'd been in here at the same time as him, when she first discovered the papers in the secret drawer in his desk, and when he'd almost shouted at her to never come into the room again.

She wondered what he thought as he spoke those words to her.

Had he, over the years, stopped seeing her as his daughter, or was it fear that had caused him to behave that way, fear that she would find out the truth?

There were still so many things she didn't know or understand, but for now, she needed to concentrate on the job at hand, which was learning as much as she could about the smooth running of the household that she was going to be in charge of.

Mrs. Harris waited until Anna sat down before sitting down herself and pulling out her small notebook. They then went through everything that needed to be organised. When Anna stumbled, not knowing what to say next, Mrs. Harris gently prompted her with the next item on the list. It wasn't long before it was all done, and just as they were finishing up, Eliza walked into the room.

Anna watched as Mrs. Harris and Eliza seemed to exchange a look, and she wondered whether Eliza had deliberately left her to go through these things with Mrs. Harris on her own.

"Thank you, Miss Anna," Mrs. Harris said and bobbed a small curtsy before leaving the two sisters in the study together.

"How did that go?" Eliza asked, and with that question, Anna knew for sure that Eliza's absence had been deliberate.

"It went surprisingly well," Anna said, smiling. "Mrs. Harris was very helpful."

. . .

"I told you she would be," said Eliza. "She took the news very positively, and I was encouraged when she assured me that she would help in whatever way she could to support you. I know that in the past your relationship with her has been strained, but I don't believe that is the cause. She doesn't dislike you," Eliza said.

"Well, I don't know why it was," Anna said, "but I have to admit she's been nothing but helpful, and certainly today, as we went through everything on her list, I felt her support in your absence."

Eliza smiled.
"I'm glad to hear it. You know that was my plan," she chuckled.

"Yes, I thought so," Anna said.

"I know things are difficult with some of the servants," Eliza said, "but it will change and it will get better. I'm sure that if you were to mention anything to Mrs. Harris, she would deal with any behaviour that wasn't appropriate."

Remembering how Mrs Harris used to deal with her previously, Anna wouldn't wish a reprimand on anyone.

"I'm sure it's just a misunderstanding," Anna reassured Eliza. "It will take a while for everyone to get used to such a different situation," she said carefully. "It's taking me long enough to feel that I belong in the role that you insist I step into. It's no surprise that there may be tensions, but we will get used to it together."

Eliza was constantly amazed at Anna's maturity and the way she dealt with everything.

When she spoke about it to Lord Whitfield, he'd laughed.

"Don't you see how alike the two of you are?" he said. "The way she's dealing with this is so similar to how you dealt with the difficulties you found yourself in after your father passed away."

. . .

When he'd said the words, she couldn't disagree, and she smiled at Anna, pleased at finding a similarity between the two of them.

Anna smiled back at Eliza, for the first time starting to feel secure in the responsibilities that she had and in her place in the household.

CHAPTER 21

Anna looked at the papers in front of her; it was a list of all the debtors still owed. Lord Whitfield had said he would pay everyone in full but needed to understand the full extent of the situation first.

Anna had worked her way through Lord Harrow's desk, trying to find everything she could.

She tried to speak to Lord Harrow's advisor, but he'd been less than helpful.

It seemed that while Eliza and Lord Whitfield felt taking over the running of the household was Anna's birthright, many others outside the family questioned it.

Lord Harrow's advisor hadn't been the only one.

Even though Mr. Percy had been paid in full, he

still found a reason to come to the house and leer at Anna, making it clear that, as far as he was concerned, she didn't belong and her place was in the kitchen where it had always been.

Mrs. Harris had led him out the door as quickly as possible, and Anna had never been more grateful to see the stern look on the housekeeper's face.

It hadn't stopped Mr. Percy from giving her one last look of disgust before he was led away.

While Lord Harrow's advisor hadn't been so obvious, Anna knew that was exactly what he thought too.

Lord Whitfield had reassured her that he would deal with any of these men in the future, but Anna felt that she had to stand up to these challenges herself if she was ever to be accepted by the social circle she now found herself in. She couldn't hide behind Lord Whitfield or Eliza's skirts.

Eliza had made it clear that she would stand by her side, showing a united front to any who would question Anna's entitlement to be the lady of the house, even if it meant admitting to the embarrassment of her father's behaviour in the past.

. . .

Anna was always grateful for Eliza's support and that of Lord Whitfield. The two of them made such a strong couple, and it was clear how much they had come to love each other.

Eliza knew that while their support would continue once they were married, Anna would be in the house on her own for now. She tried not to think too hard about that and all that it might mean.

She looked down once again at the papers in front of her. She was thankful for the education that Lord Harrow had given her; without it, she wouldn't have been able to make sense of any of what she was looking at. But she could see clearly who was owed and how much.

She knew that paying off the debt was the first challenge. The biggest challenge of all would be to secure the continuing finances to keep the household running and ensure that everyone was paid, so the servants who knew this as their home would still have that security.

She heard a small tap on the door and, when she looked up, saw Lord Whitfield walking through it.

"It suits you," he said, smiling.

· · ·

Anna rose, laughing softly.

"I'm not sure," she said. "My place here feels far too big for me to fill, and Eliza has done such a wonderful job before me. I'm not sure I could ever really do it justice."

"You doubt yourself unnecessarily," Lord Whitfield said. "Eliza assures me that you're doing a wonderful job at keeping everything running, and from the looks of it, with you sitting at the desk, you seem to have a handle on everything in here as well."

"I have the list of debtors, certainly. There are quite a lot, and I greatly appreciate your willingness to clear everything. I know that you're doing it for Eliza, but I'm also very grateful."

"Certainly, in the beginning, I was doing it for Eliza," Lord Whitfield agreed. "But I've come to care for you, Anna, and anything that I can do to help you, to guide you, to make things easier for you, you only need to ask. I feel that paying Lord Harrow's debts is just the beginning of what is required for this household to run smoothly."

Anna nodded.

"It was just what I was thinking as you arrived," she agreed. "Certainly, I will need a lot of help trying to make sense of all of this."

"And you won't be doing it on your own," Lord Whitfield assured her. "I'll be here whenever you need me for as long as it takes." Then he smiled at her. "But I don't think it will be as long as you think, Anna."

Anna sighed. She wasn't sure she agreed, but she was grateful for his encouragement.

"Why don't you leave that all with me now," he said. "I'm sure Eliza has wedding plans she'd like to discuss with you."

. . .

Anna got up from the desk gratefully and walked out of the study looking for her sister.

Eliza was in the sitting room, looking at materials and discussing guest lists with Mrs. Harris.

"Oh good, you're here," she said as Anna walked through the door. "We need to decide on the material for your dress for our wedding."

It was yet another thing that Anna hadn't thought about.

While she assumed she would be invited, of course, she hadn't even considered that she would be going as Eliza's sister, not as a servant nor even as someone she was friendly with.

It completely changed her role at the wedding too.

Of course, it was Eliza's day, but Anna was aware that it would be the first big social engagement where everyone would see her and Eliza as sisters. When she'd mentioned this to Eliza the other day, she had the thought waved away.

. . .

"I want everyone to see that we're sisters," Eliza had said. "We are sisters, and everyone we know should see how proud of that I am."

Her words had warmed Anna's heart, but she still struggled with the idea of it all. Eliza had reassured her that she would go through everything she needed to know about the behaviour of polite society.

"I promise you, Anna," she said, "you will not feel out of place. If anyone tries to behave in any way other than respectfully towards you, they will be asked to leave. It's not only me saying this but Lord Whitfield also. You are part of our family, and we will not put up with anyone treating you as anything different."

True to his word, Lord Whitfield repaid all the debts that Lord Harrow had accrued. He went to speak to each creditor individually, explained the situation, and paid them in full.

Each of them had already received a letter from

Eliza in the past, and Lord Harrow had behaved towards them as they had behaved towards her in response to her request for understanding. To those who had been gracious and offered help, Lord Whitfield returned the favour in kind. However, to those who hadn't, he made clear his disapproval of their behaviour.

Both Eliza and Anna felt protected by him, and the close family bond that had been growing between them became even stronger as he showed his support for them both. But there remained the challenge of securing future finances to keep the household running and to ensure Anna could live a comfortable and secure life.

Additionally, there was the lesser challenge of dealing with the whispers of gossips who couldn't seem to help but talk negatively. Lord Whitfield, as an older gentleman, had learned to ignore them, but he knew that the comments being made would hurt Anna, and so he was even more determined to help her succeed.

. . .

He visited most days and helped her understand what needed to be done to secure her financial future. Now that the debt was completely cleared, they were all determined never to sink so low again, and together, the three of them devised a plan.

As everyone in the household saw how hard Anna worked alongside Lord Whitfield and Miss Eliza, their respect for her grew. Anna knew it wasn't just that which changed their behaviour towards her; she was aware that Mrs Harris must have spoken to each and every one of them. However, instead of her usual reproachful manner, Mrs Harris seemed to handle any issues gently.

Anna wondered how much Mrs Jones had influenced Mrs Harris because the change in her seemed very similar to the cook's caring ways. Anna missed her time speaking with Mrs Jones. She was so busy with her new responsibilities that she hadn't had the opportunity to find out what Mrs Jones thought about Anna's new role.

She knew things would calm down, especially now that Lord Whitfield was being so supportive. Once they did, Anna was determined to visit Mrs

Jones and spend time with the woman who had always been like a mother to her.

For now, though, Anna, with Eliza and Lord Whitfield by her side, was starting to feel a sense of hope for what she might be able to achieve, and she was encouraged by how positively the household was responding.

As Lord Whitfield quietly dealt with the gossips, Anna and Eliza focused on the future.

CHAPTER 22

Anna pulled out the letters her mother, Mary had written.

They were creased and tear-stained from all the times she had read and reread them since they had been discovered.

Everything in them broke her heart.

While the love Mary had for Lord Harrow shone through, Anna felt that she still didn't know who her mother truly was.

She had been so busy taking on her new role and all the responsibilities that came with it that she had made no progress in making sense of her mother's diary and letters. They were all one-sided and showed just a small season of her mother's life and only a small part of who she was.

. . .

As Anna had stepped into her new position in the household, she often wondered how much of herself was similar to her mother. Every now and then, she would see a glimpse of Eliza in how she handled something, and she assumed that this trait was inherited from Lord Harrow.

She wasn't sure how she felt about that. She was still trying to come to terms with how he had behaved towards her mother.

Of course, she had only come to the conclusions she had about him because the only documents she was reading were those her mother had written. She longed to find a more complete story about the two of them and about how she had come to be.

She had considered asking Eliza a few times, but she felt that her younger half-sister had already done so much for her. To hand over the house without a second thought and to stand by her in support was more than she could ever have expected and more than she deserved.

She might be Lord Harrow's oldest child, but it didn't change the fact that she was illegitimate and entitled to nothing. Eliza's behaviour was all the more gracious because of that.

. . .

ANNA KNEW that it was time to start the day, and after another quick read-through of the letters, she folded them up and put them back into the drawer by her bed. She looked around her bedroom; it was a far cry from the one she had grown up in.

Once Eliza had decided that Anna was now the lady of the house, she had insisted that Anna needed a bedroom befitting that position.

Truthfully, Eliza had tried to get Anna to move bedrooms as soon as she told her the truth about who her father was, but Anna had been unable to comprehend it all at that point. Now, as she looked around the bedroom, amazed at how pretty it was, she knew she would never stop being thankful for the life she now found herself living.

SHE WAS UP and out of bed before the servant girl who usually came in to open her curtains had arrived. She opened the curtains herself and looked out onto the street below, which was only just starting to wake up. It wasn't just the bedroom she was grateful for but the fact that she now had a home she never had to worry about losing.

There had been a time when she had wondered if she might find herself like many other young girls without family to protect them, on the street, having to do the most unthinkable things to survive.

The thought of it made her shudder.

No, that was no longer something she had to consider, and as long as she drew breath, she would make sure that none of the other girls—the servants who lived and worked in this house—would have to concern themselves with that kind of future either.

When she walked downstairs, she was surprised at how quiet the house still was. She was used to waking early, before anyone else. It had been so much easier to get everything ready for the lord and lady when there was nobody else about, and she supposed that rising early was now a habit.

She could hear faint noises coming from the kitchen, and she walked towards it, taking in the smell of bread wafting towards her. When she walked through the door, she saw that Mrs Jones was on her own, preparing for the day ahead. She turned when she heard Anna and smiled warmly. It felt like a welcoming warm hug.

· · ·

It was Anna's first memory, and seeing it reminded her how much she had missed spending time with the older woman.

"Sit down, lass," Mrs Jones said. "Let me pour you some tea."

Before Anna realised it, she was sat at the table, a cup of tea in her hand, surprised at how familiar it all felt.

Mrs Jones beamed at her.

"It's so good to see you, and look how far you've come. It's only right," she said.

Her comment piqued Anna's interest.

"What do you mean, 'it's only right'?" Anna pressed.

Mrs Jones looked flustered. Her cheeks started to turn pink, and Anna knew it wasn't just from the warmth in the kitchen. She realised that the older woman knew something—something about Anna.

"Oh, nothing," Mrs Jones said. "Don't mind the words of a silly old woman."

. . .

But Anna wouldn't let it go.

"Please, Mrs Jones," she said. "You always told me that you would tell me more when I was older, when it was the right time. Surely it's the right time now. You've always worked here, haven't you? Surely you knew my mother. You must have known her," Anna asked.

Mrs Jones couldn't bring herself to look at Anna as she nodded.

"Please, tell me about her," Anna requested simply.

"Well," said Mrs Jones, "I did know your mother, Mary. I knew her when she first came to work here. She was a pretty thing; you look a lot like her," she said as she finally looked up and smiled. "You remind me of her very much. She was intelligent and kind, a quick learner, and she would do anything for anyone. She had a wonderful sense of humour; she loved to laugh and to make those around her laugh too. She always found joy in anything and everything."

. . .

Mrs Jones paused for a moment, and the smile that lit up her eyes began to fade.

"I imagine that's why his lordship fell in love with her."

The mention of Lord Harrow felt like an arrow in Anna's heart.

"He did love her, you know," Mrs Jones continued. "Not long after she started working here, it was clear that she'd won his heart. They were almost inseparable, which was hard to do given that it wasn't right for the two of them to be together. He hid it as best he could from his parents, you know, but in the end, he loved her so much that he didn't want to hide it. And that's when the troubles started."

Mrs Jones stopped talking and shook her head. Anna could see the tears start to well in the old woman's eyes.

"From then on, it was heartbreak for both of them," she said. "But of course, by then you were already on the way. Your mother, Mary, she'd been sent away. His lordship's parents thought that once she wasn't here, he would come to his senses. But of course, that's not how love works, is it? And Mary, she never gave up hope. She always thought that his lordship would come to her eventually, that he would fulfil his promises to her. But he never got the chance to."

Anna looked at Mrs Jones, surprised.

"What do you mean?" she asked.

"Well, your mother wrote, but he was never given those letters," Mrs Jones explained. "The house staff were told that he was to have nothing given to him that wasn't read by his mother and father first. I saw those letters arrive; I recognised her handwriting. But we all had to do the right thing. It was made clear that if we went against their wishes, we'd be out, and none of us wanted to be on the streets. I feel terrible saying it to you, Miss Anna. Perhaps things would have been so much different if one of us could have been brave enough. But we were all much younger then, and his lordship's father ruled with a rod of iron. We knew that he meant every word of that threat. And so, his lordship never got the letters that your mother wrote. He didn't find them until quite a while after, and by then, poor Mary had given up all hope and gone to be with the angels. But once he knew, he did his best for you. He did,"

Mrs Jones reached across, taking Anna's hand in hers and patting it before reaching over and stroking her cheek gently.

"He didn't know how to do the right thing, but he thought that if you had a place here to work, you would have a home forever and at least you'd be safe. He couldn't tell his parents, so he made something up. I don't know the story he told them in the end, but I do know that he tried his best. He tried his best for you, and he loved your mother very much."

Anna couldn't stop the tears from rolling down her cheeks. It wasn't quite the complete story she thought she'd hear, but in some ways, it brought peace and the beginning of understanding of her father's behaviour.

The fact that he had loved her mother and had tried to do his best by her was the beginning of her finding acceptance in who she was and how she had come to be here. Perhaps it was a story she would never know in full, and maybe what she knew would be enough.

. . .

"It was Mrs Harris who brought you here, and I was shocked," Mrs Jones continued. "She was close friends with your mother and she was determined that his lordship would know you and take responsibility."

All this time, Anna had felt the watchful eyes of Mrs Harris always upon her, somehow always there to castigate her in some way.

"She's always cared for you deeply," Mrs Jones said as Anna shook her head in disbelief.

Mrs Jones chuckled.

"I know she doesn't do it in a way that you would understand, but she's always wanted the very best for you. And I know that when Miss Eliza found out that you were her sister, Mrs Harris hoped that you would finally live the life that you deserved. To see how Miss Eliza has been, well, it has made Mrs Harris and I both proud of the young woman that she has become. And as we see you blossom, we're proud of you too, Miss Anna."

. . .

Anna felt like her heart would burst from her chest.

For so many years, she had felt so alone, yet unknowingly she had been surrounded by people who loved and cared for her, who knew who she was and were waiting for the moment when she might be able to step into the life they felt she had always deserved.

Knowing that helped her to start to lay to rest the mystery of who she was.

CHAPTER 23

*E*liza blushed as she overheard the two young women talking amongst themselves. It was obvious from their words that they didn't realise she was standing behind them.

As much as she wanted to be brave and butt into the conversation, she instead took a step back as quietly as possible so that they wouldn't hear her and turn around to see her standing there. She was only thankful that Anna had been too busy to come out with her today.

Lord Whitfield had mentioned that he had been dealing with some gossip that had risen up in their social circle. Eliza had believed, naively it seems now, that dealing with it meant it was no longer happening, but that wasn't the case.

She had spent so many years in the townhouse, almost alone with her father the only person to keep her company, that she had become unaware of how cruel some people's words could be. There had been times, of course, when she had heard servants gossip, but she assumed that was more to do with their standing in life; she believed people like her would never stoop to such terrible behaviour.

She felt ashamed for thinking like that, especially because gossip was something she had never engaged in. Anna had grown up believing herself to be no more than a lowly servant, and today it had been proven to her again that such behaviour was rife among people of any standing.

She walked over to where Lord Whitfield had been waiting for her.

"Did you get what you wanted?" he asked.

She shook her head, and he raised an eyebrow in question.

"Not here," she said. "Let's go home."

They walked over to his carriage, and he helped her up. Once they were inside, he took her hands into his own.

"Tell me, my love," he said gently.

"I don't understand why people are so cruel and unkind," she said. "I just heard two young women, they can't have been much older than Anna, saying such terrible things about our family. It breaks my heart. I thought by now that all the gossip would have been finished with."

Lord Whitfield sighed.

"I'm afraid that some people will always have something unkind to say, my dear," he said. "But we have the ability to rise above it, to stand together, to support each other, and to know that we are doing the right thing. You did the right thing, Eliza, by handing over the house to Anna. Even if we weren't getting married, it still would have been a good thing to do. You should never be ashamed of that."

Eliza nodded, knowing he was right, grateful again for his wisdom and support.

"What would I do without you?" she smiled.

"You'd be snapped up by some handsome young man who would whisk you off your feet. But you know he would never love you as much as I do."

Eliza leaned back and rested her head on his shoulder.

The care she had felt for him was now a deep love.

When she thought back to how worried she had been at the idea of the marriage arranged between them, it surprised her. While she didn't for a moment think that her father had chosen Lord Whitfield because he thought he would be a good match for his daughter, it had certainly turned out that way. She would never have been able to face all the storms that had come her way if she hadn't had him by her side.

"People will get used to how things are," he reassured her. "Even now, some of those who doubted Anna have changed their view. Those people who matter will see the truth for what it is, and they are the only ones we need to take into consideration. In the end, we're a family, and we stand together. We support each other, and we care for each other. I see Anna as a sister that I care for deeply. It will just take some time. Have patience, my love."

"I shall do my best," said Eliza, and they laughed, knowing that patience wasn't one of her strongest traits.

But she knew that her husband-to-be was right.

Anna had proven herself over and over again in the running of the household.

Certainly, she had the wisdom of Lord Whitfield to begin with, guiding her, but it hadn't been long before Anna had taken over the running of almost everything to do with the house.

She had the support of Mrs Harris and Mrs

Jones, and because of that, the servants, even those who struggled to begin with, were her biggest allies. She knew that just as there was negative gossip going around, there were also the whispers of the servants sharing with their friends and family how much better the household was to work in, how it was now starting to be a place of joy once again. Eliza knew that over time, those positive whispers would outweigh any negative ones. She just didn't want to see Anna hurt by any unkind words.

What took Eliza by surprise the most was that the gossip was most often about her and Anna. It seemed not many people had negative words to say about her father and his own behaviour.

Of course, there had been comments made about the debts she had had to deal with and the fact that he had brought them almost to financial ruin, but it seemed that had now been forgotten.

It was just that a woman was now running the household, and one who had once been a servant, that seemed to raise eyebrows.

She shook the thoughts from her mind. There was no point in continuing to think about it, she decided.

Lord Whitfield was right; there would always be people who had unkind words to say, but over time, the fact that the three of them stood together, supporting each other, would show anyone who bothered to look past the gossip how things really were.

By the time the carriage had pulled up, Eliza realised that they were at his house and not her own. It seemed that so close to their wedding day, he already saw this as their home. It made her smile and warmed her heart.

"Oh," he said, realising where they were.

Eliza laughed.

"I wanted to see the children anyway," she said, and he helped her down from the carriage and led her inside.

Anna wasn't immune to the gossip; it wasn't that she wasn't aware of it, and when it reached her, it did hurt, but only for a moment.

She had been surrounded by gossip of some sort all of her life. Mostly, it had been servants passing information on regarding her lack of a mother and wondering who her father might be.

It was ironic that the gossip was about the same thing but for different reasons now.

Everybody knew who her father was and her mother, and the fact that they had been so far apart socially. But even that wasn't the direct cause of the gossip. Most of it was about the fact that she was now running a household after having been nothing more than a servant herself not that long ago.

Though no one could seem to fault her behaviour or how she was running the household, it seemed everybody was waiting for her to fail. There was no denying that. But as she continued to find success in small ways, she knew that eventually, they would find something else to talk about.

Somebody else, probably, she thought, and she regretted the small sense of relief she felt at the idea of that. She had always disliked gossip, whoever it was about.

But she felt stronger and stronger each day.

Her conversation with Mrs Jones had brought a peace within her that had helped her more than she ever thought possible.

Since then, she'd spoken to Mrs Harris as well, and the two older women had been nothing but supportive. Added to that was her sister Eliza and her soon-to-be brother-in-law, Lord Whitfield.

No matter what anybody else might say, Anna knew that she finally had a family.

She understood that Lord Harrow had indeed tried to do his best for her.

She still felt sad about how it all ended and

couldn't help but wonder whether things could have been different. But she knew that if they had been, then Lord Harrow would never have married Eliza's mother, and she would never have had a sister. She probably would never have found herself here, living this life that she was beginning to love. Things would have been very different.

From the conversations that she had with Mrs Jones, she knew that Lord Harrow's parents would never have accepted her mother, and it would have been Lord Harrow who'd had to go and live in some squalid place.

She shuddered at the idea that that could have been her life. While he might have placed her as a servant, things could have been so much worse, and she reminded herself of that daily.

It was that thought that caused her to strive to build a solid foundation for her future and the future of the household. She knew that her actions were changing the atmosphere that everyone lived and worked in every day. She could feel the positivity, and she could feel the support. As the household recovered financially, she knew that she was building a better life for everybody.

CHAPTER 24

The house was abuzz with planning and preparations for Eliza and Lord Whitfield's wedding. They had been organising it for a few months, but now that the day was almost upon them, it seemed like there was so much more to get ready.

Eliza could feel butterflies in her stomach, not because she was concerned about marrying Lord Whitfield, but because she wanted everything to be perfect. Anna had noticed how nervous she was feeling.

"Let me finish these last preparations for you, Eliza. You just enjoy the excitement of getting married and know that when you turn up, everything will be perfect," Anna said.

Eliza was grateful to have Anna take it all off her hands. There was something wonderful about knowing she had a sister she could entrust with such an important day.

They decided that their wedding ceremony would be a modest one, and because Lord Whitfield had proposed in his garden, Eliza had suggested that they celebrate the wedding breakfast there.

They would marry in the small local church with just their closest friends and family before all coming together to celebrate in the garden that held such wonderful memories for Eliza.

Anna was to be her only bridesmaid.

When she'd first asked her, it was almost as if she was going to refuse.

"I can't possibly," Anna said, but when Eliza reached out her hands to her, she watched as Anna's shoulders straightened.

. . .

"Of course I can," she said. "It would be an honour."

Eliza's friends were almost non-existent now, and Anna was the closest person in her life. Having her stand by her side was all that she needed.

When the wedding day came, Eliza knew that she didn't need to worry about a single thing. Anna came to her bedroom in the morning, and the two of them helped each other get ready. A few of the servants hovered around, waiting to be asked to do something, but the two young women were enjoying the time they had to spend together, knowing it would be the last time they would have a moment like this.

"I'm so happy for you, Eliza," Anna said, "but I have to be truthful and tell you how sad it will be not having you here with me."

"I won't be far," Eliza said. "Now that we've found each other, I hope that we will spend as much time together as we can, even when we are both married women."

Anna laughed.

"I think that's a long way ahead for me," she said. "I have too much to do here to be thinking about a husband."

Eliza chuckled.

"Sometimes they arrive when you least expect it," she said and smiled, thinking about her own beloved and how something that had started as an arrangement had become a love story.

When they were both ready, they made their way downstairs and out to the carriage that waited for them. They were both helped inside and driven to the church.

Because Eliza didn't have a father to walk her down the aisle, she asked Anna if she would walk down with her.

It was yet another opportunity to show those who were there how important her sister was to her.

As they walked down the aisle towards where Lord Whitfield waited, Anna gave her sister a small hug before placing her hands into his and stepping away. She was sure she had seen the glisten of a tear in his eye as he watched Eliza walk towards him, seeing how beautiful she was.

The ceremony was short but heartfelt, and by the time they got back to Lord Whitfield's house, Eliza's new home, everyone was ready to celebrate with them.

Lord Whitfield's children were there, and as Eliza looked around, she saw how perfect everything looked. She looked over to where Anna stood and mouthed a thank you to her. It was everything she could have hoped for.

Anna looked around at all the people who had come to the wedding, and she watched as each one seemed to look at her with newfound respect and regard.

Finally, she thought, she was starting to be accepted. She knew that part of that was because of Eliza and Lord Whitfield and everything they had done to support her, but she also knew that she supported them too.

Watching the two of them together, she was grateful to have them in her life and was so thankful that they'd found each other. Their love for each other shone, and Anna hoped that one day she might find that love for herself. T

hey sat down at the wedding table as they were served their meal and once they'd finished eating, Lord Whitfield turned to Anna.

"Thank you, Anna, for this. It's perfect, and I know that Eliza feels the same."

Eliza nodded in agreement, and the three of them smiled and looked around, feeling the love and support of everyone who was there to share the day with them.

"To new beginnings," said Lord Whitfield, raising his glass to the two young women.

"To new beginnings," they both echoed, knowing that looked very different for each of them.

. . .

The End

Printed in Great Britain
by Amazon